PRAISE FO

"Chiavaroli delights with this homage to Louisa May Alcott's *Little Women*, featuring a time-slip narrative of two women connected across centuries."

PUBLISHERS WEEKLY on *The Orchard House*

"As a longtime fan of Louisa May Alcott's *Little Women*, I was eager to read *The Orchard House*.... [It] invited me in, served me tea, and held me enthralled with its compelling tale."

LORI BENTON, Christy Award-winning author of *The King's Mercy*

"Captivating from the first page....Steeped in timeless truths and served with skill, *The Tea Chest* is sure to be savored by all who read it."

*JOCELYN GREEN,* Christy Award-winning author of *Between Two Shores*

"*The Hidden Side* is a beautiful tale that captures the timeless struggles of the human heart."

JULIE CANTRELL, *New York Times* Bestselling author of *Perennials*

"First novelist Chiavaroli's historical tapestry will provide a satisfying summer read for fans of Kristy Cambron and Lisa Wingate."

*LIBRARY JOURNAL* on *Freedom's Ring*

"*The Edge of Mercy* is most definitely one for the keeper shelf. "

LINDSAY HARREL, author of *The Secrets of Paper and Ink*

# WHERE MEMORIES AWAIT

## HEIDI CHIAVAROLI

Hope Creek Publishers LLC

Visit Heidi Chiavaroli at heidichiavaroli.com

Hope Creek Publishers LLC

Cover Design by Carpe Librum Book Design

Author Photograph by Marla Darius, copyright © 2018. All rights reserved.

Edited by Melissa Jagears

Scripture quotations are taken from the New International Version.

*Where Memories Await* is a work of fiction. Where real people, events, establishments, organizations, or locales appear, they are used fictitiously. All other elements of the novel are drawn from the author's imagination.

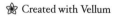 Created with Vellum

ALSO BY HEIDI CHIAVAROLI

The Orchard House

The Tea Chest

The Hidden Side

Freedom's Ring

The Edge of Mercy

**The Orchard House Bed and Breakfast Series**

Where Grace Appears

Where Hope Begins

Where Love Grows

Where Memories Await

*To Grammy*

The ghosts of my past show themselves on Christmas Eve more than any other night of the year.

I drag in a deep breath and place the tiny sheep figurine from my manger back in its place. It stands out from the rest of the set—slightly bigger, not as intricately carved as the other figures.

That never mattered to me.

My chest aches and I lean back in my bedroom chair and close my eyes, praying for relief from the hauntings.

A knock sounds at my door.

"Come in."

The door creaks open and my niece Josie pokes her mass of chestnut hair around the corner. "Hey, Aunt Pris. Mom's heading to the church early to help with the pageant. She wondered if you were okay going with me and Tripp?"

"I suppose."

She enters my room, coming closer. She looks pretty tonight, has taken time to do her hair and makeup.

"You feeling okay?"

"As well as I can for my eighty-two years." Aches and pains are a normal part of life now, especially in these cold Maine winters. "I'll be out in a few minutes."

But Josie doesn't leave. Always my pesky niece, this one. But she has spunk. Reminds me of myself back in the day. "If you don't feel well enough to come, God will understand. You can join us for carols and food after if you'd like. Lizzie and Asher are playing us their new song."

The thought that she doesn't want me at the service scrapes painfully across my heart. "Girl, I haven't missed a Christmas Eve service in eighty-one years, and I don't intend to begin now. I'm fine. Only keeping company with my memories." I allow my gaze to fall on that sheep, attempting to shove away the ghosts. I inwardly curse when Josie approaches my nightstand and caresses the object of my attention. The girl doesn't miss a trick.

"Tell me why you like sheep so much, Aunt Pris?"

She'd given me two sheep figurines when we opened The Orchard House Bed and Breakfast. One could make the case I was off my rocker for allowing my dead nephew's wife and children to convince me to transform my old Victorian into an inn—complete with a live-in family. But most of the time, though I didn't make it a plain fact, I considered myself blessed beyond measure.

Josie had noticed my fetish with the gentle animal during the extensive renovations Colton Contractors performed.

"Can't an old woman have any secrets?" I shouldn't snap at her. I blame it on my blasted back, sore with every breath tonight.

My tone doesn't deter her, though. She kneels at my feet. She smells like coconut and baby powder, and something in my heart threatens to burst. I am grateful for her and her siblings. For their Mum, Amos's wife. They could have abandoned me, forgotten me. Especially after my nephew died. Especially with my some-times...challenging nature. But they didn't. Instead, they've breathed new life into this old house, given me company and companionship in this last stretch of my life.

"Don't you want to share your stories, Aunt Pris? I want to hear them—we all do. Would it hurt to open up?" She nudges my arm, a teasing twinkle in her eyes. "It is Christmas Eve, after all. A time for miracles."

Christmas Eve. A time for miracles. Bleh. Too bad I only harbor sad memories.

But the girl is right. My time on earth is short. Even if I lived another twenty years, I knew from experience how fast they could fly. Or how quickly a mind slips. I think of my friend Esther. Poor dear, I am grateful her days still prove healthy. It's nights that have a way of stealing her mind. Dementia is not kind.

I glance at Josie. Would sharing my story help to make anything different, or would it only serve to open old wounds?

"Don't you have a child and a husband to be with on Christmas Eve, girl?"

She grins. "They're both taking naps." She digs out her phone. How anyone can carry those ringing, beeping contraptions around every hour of the day is beyond me. "We have more than half an hour if you feel like spilling your guts."

"As enticing as spilling out one's guts sounds, I think I shall pass."

"Then at least tell me why you like sheep so much."

So young and audacious. Why do I pretend I don't see my own dear sister in her—a different piece of Hazel was in every one of my great nieces.

My hand takes up a small tremor and I command it still, to no avail. "I don't like them."

She cocks her head to one side and speaks slow. "You don't like sheep, so you cover your bed and curtains and walls with pictures of them?"

I press my lips together. Do I want to travel this path? So

many years of keeping it bottled up...then again, do I want to take it to the grave?

"Do you know what penance is?" I ask.

"Yes, of course. It's something you pay to show you're sorry. Kind of like proving you're sorry."

"The sheep are my penance."

Her eyebrows come together, the dim light of my nightstand lamp casting divots of shadow and light on her brow. "Oh, Aunt Pris."

"Don't pity me, girl. You're the one who asked, but I refuse any show of pity. Understood?"

She nods, solemn as ever I've seen her. We remain silent—me wavering at the bridge before me, her undoubtedly wondering whether to push me to cross.

She doesn't. My heart ceases its wretched pounding.

There is a certain calm in thinking about it, I suppose. Perhaps this would be part of my penance. Dare I hope sharing would finally release me?

"Your grandmother—my sister...she loved sheep."

Josie takes in a small inhalation of breath. No wonder. The child knows nothing of her grandmother, as Amos had known nothing of his mother. I'd been close-lipped about my younger sister for nearly sixty years now. I oft wondered if the family forgot I ever knew Hazel.

"What do you know about sheep, girl?"

"Um...not much. They're kind of stupid, aren't they? And when they fall on their backs, they can't get up by themselves."

My jaw tightens, and I force it loose. "They are not stupid, Josie. But they are emotional. And yes, many times they are help-less." Another moment of quiet.

I stare at the electric candle at my window. Beyond the dark, the apple orchards of my childhood roll up a gradual hill, alive and well thanks to my nephew Bronson. The trees still standing from my youth are at the end of their fruit-bearing years. They've born witness to my entire life.

Something tells me to stop talking, but something stronger urges me forward. "Hazel was not stupid. But her emotions...well, they always seemed to get her into trouble."

*Camden, Maine*
*December, 1957*

I didn't know what mortified me more—that I'd sat through the entire scandalous film, or that I'd actually found it entertaining.

Of course, I refused to let Hazel know as much.

I tugged on my younger sister's arm, but she ignored me, turning to her friend, Dolly.

"Did you see me? I was in the green dress at the graduation dance. Barry was right next to me."

Barry. Wonderful. Now my sister thought she was on a first-name basis with a movie star because she was an extra in one film.

Dolly grabbed my sister's arm. "Did you completely flip your lid being that close to him?"

"On the inside, I was a mess. He's an absolute dreamboat!"

"Hazel, curfew's in ten. We have to leave," I reminded.

My sister kissed her friend on the cheek. "Have to split, Dol. See you at school on Monday?"

"Planning committee for senior prom—don't forget this time."

"I won't." Hazel promised Dolly before we slipped out of the theatre. I pulled the hood of my parka over my head and hoped to high heaven no one from church or the yacht club would see us. The movie dealt with the unspeakable—rape, incest, adultery, and abortion. Topics my parents would rather die than acknowledge.

I grabbed my sister's arm and walked fast with my head down.

"Pris, what's the rush? Can't you let me bask in my glory?"

I rolled my eyes. "You were in the background of three scenes for a total of forty-five seconds. It's a great experience, but I don't know how much glory you'll be getting from it."

And only because the heavens enjoyed proving me wrong, Roger McClintock came around my sister's other side and flung an arm over her shoulder. "Hazel, you looked great. *Really* great. You're practically a star."

Considering the only part of my sister that had been shown during the film was her back half, I didn't have to guess what part of her Roger considered great. I wanted to be offended on her behalf, but it was so hard with her standing there smiling, her blonde bobbed hair swishing back and forth, a slight blush on her cheeks.

"Thanks, Roger."

"Hey, a bunch of us are grabbing a pop at Fat Berry's. Want to come?"

"Oh..." Hazel looked at me, and then longingly at Roger. I shook my head, hating my role as the older sister but knowing Mum and Daddy expected me to wrangle her home by curfew.

Hazel blew out an unladylike breath that fanned her hair. "Sorry, Roger. I have to get going. Next time?"

He pinched her on the cheek. "Sure, kid. See you Monday." He walked back toward the theater.

We veered left toward the harbor in the direction of our home, Orchard House. The wind coming off the water chilled my face.

I shivered. "There's something about that guy that gives me the heebie-jeebies."

"Everything about guys gives you the heebie-jeebies."

"That's not true. It's the way he's pinching your cheek and slinging his arm around you...it's too familiar."

"Don't be a wet rag, Pris. You're too serious. That's how guys are sometimes, you know?"

"Not all guys." Ed wasn't—not by a long shot.

"Well, how would you know? You never get out enough."

I bristled at the comment. She'd already written me off as an old maid.

"What about Raymond?" Hazel continued. "What's wrong with him? He's handsome enough, and you know it would tickle Mum and Dad's fancy if you'd give him a chance."

I wrinkled my nose at the thought of Raymond Hitch, Vice President of First Camden National Bank. "I refuse to degrade myself or whoever my future husband might be by judging him by physical appearance and wallet alone. Raymond doesn't have much else to prove admirable beyond that, I'm afraid."

Hazel grinned. Moonlight shone off the sapphire pendant at her throat. "I think you read too many books."

To our right, the harbor sparkled, reflecting the multitude of stars splashing down from the Maine nighttime sky. I kept my gaze on the glimmering body of water, unable to meet my sister's probing stare.

I swallowed. "You think I should marry him, don't you?"

"Not while you're in love with Ed Colton, I don't."

I slapped her arm. "Hazel!"

"What? Is it a secret?"

"*I* thought it was."

"And I suppose you sneaking out your window at night to meet him is a secret, too? You're not fooling anyone, dragging me home for curfew just so you can sneak back out to meet your beau."

I stumbled for words. My sister flashed me a wicked grin.

"Don't worry, I actually find it terribly romantic. Camden society's wealthiest daughter falls for lowly construction laborer. It has the makings of a Hollywood movie, don't you think?"

I cringed. "Please don't say anything, especially to Mum and Daddy. Besides, it's not serious. It's..."

Hazel raised her eyebrows. "It's...what?"

I swiped a frustrated hand through the air. "It's no one's business!" I walked faster, angry at myself for not being more careful with my after-dark escapades.

Hazel caught up with me. "Oh no, you don't. It's not fair that you're keeping me from my fun but going behind Mum and Daddy's backs with Ed. At least give me the scoop on what's going on between you two."

We passed the Village Green where our candle-lit church perched in the middle of town, embracing everything old and historic and New England. Beside it, a life-sized Nativity scene with a single yellow bulb hung above Mary and Joseph's heads. I remember Hazel clamoring to see the set after church each Sunday when she was little. When Mum and Daddy weren't looking, she'd reach out and pet the plastic sheep, a grin wide on her face.

My silence lasted as we passed Harbor Park, the library ahead with quaint Christmas candles lighting the windows. I stopped at the building, the silver light of the moon splashing off the stone stairs of the library's courtyard amphitheater. "Didn't I keep your secret this past summer? If Mum and Daddy knew any part of you was in that film, they'd have a fit."

*Peyton Place* had been the talk of the town, and everyone had an opinion. The book, published a year before by Gloria Metalious, was nothing short of racy, and many held the view that the filming of the movie had no such place in our conservative little town.

"I appreciate you keeping my secret, and I'm donating half of the money I made toward the new hospital. Isn't that a worthy endeavor?"

"Of course, but—"

"And I have another secret for you. Only you must tell me more about you and Ed." Hazel's green eyes seared right through me, pleading. I'd never been able to refuse her much—whether it was an ice cream at Bunny's Café when we were younger, or skating at Hosmer Pond, or skiing at the Snow Bowl, more recently.

But no, not this time.

"I don't want to be a keeper of any more of your secrets, Hazel. They always end up being so much trouble for me."

My sister was uncharacteristically silent before she chose to speak. "I want to tell you this one, Priscilla. I need to."

It was the use of my full name that caught me. My knees trembled. "What—what's wrong?"

"Nothing's wrong. In fact, something is incredibly right."

My stomach relaxed. "Okay, then. Share your good news."

She shook her head. "You first. You promised."

"No, I didn't! You always have a way of flipping things around."

We continued our walk. Hazel lengthened her stride, gave me a sly grin. "Ed's cute."

I set my mouth firm, stoic.

"A girl could drown in those eyes," she continued. "He kind of looks like Marlon Brando."

My bottom lip quivered. "He's not only a handsome face to look at. He's incredibly smart and capable."

Hazel clutched my elbow and jumped up and down beside me. "It *is* true, then. You are real gone. Tell me everything. He's loved you forever—ever since the third grade when he socked Billy Windle in the eye for kissing you on the playground. When did you two start seeing one another?"

A smile tugged at my lips. I couldn't help it. Ed *was* a dreamboat, and I'd been quiet for so long about him. Only Esther, my best friend whose family lived on the third floor of our Victorian as they worked our orchards and kept house, knew anything of my relationship with Ed. "This past summer."

She squealed, encouraging me onward, even as I felt foolish for indulging in such girlish babble.

"I was going into the library and noticed a truck with its keys in the door. I brought them to the circulation desk and left a note saying how I found them. Turns out he tracked me down, insisted on thanking me by taking me out for an ice cream."

Hazel hung on my every word. "And?"

"And...I'd always turned him down in the past, but I don't know—there was something different this time. When I asked him why he was at the library, he said he was taking out business books, that he wanted to open his own construction business one day. Hazel, I always thought Ed was just a goofy kid, but I never saw him—like really saw him—until a few months ago. He's...amazing."

Hazel's dreamy-eyed gaze dissolved into solemn worry. "Mum and Dad will blow a gasket."

I dragged in a breath and shrugged. "It's 1957. If a twenty-year-old girl can't decide who she wants to love now, I don't see how society has made any progress at all."

Hazel threw her arms around me. "You're absolutely right, Sis, and I'm so glad to hear you say that."

I pulled back, cocked my head. "You think Mum and Daddy will understand?"

She laughed. "Absolutely not, but I'm still cheering you on. When are you going to tell them?"

I shook my head. "I'm not sure. Ed and I haven't talked much about the future."

"They're set on Raymond, so better start sowing seeds against that idea before it's too late."

Too late?

We continued onto High Street, and started up the drive of Orchard House, decorated with white lights and greenery for the Christmas season. Esther's family had done a beautiful job of it beneath Mum's instruction.

"Your turn." I huddled deeper into my parka as a wind came off the harbor, sweeping over my family's apple orchards.

"Hmm?"

"Your secret."

Hazel stopped walking but didn't look at me. "I'm leaving, Pris."

"What?"

"I'm leaving Camden. I've been writing to Jimmy—remember him? I met him on the set this past summer."

Jimmy? I wracked my brain for an identity to go with the name. "Wait...not that greaser cameraman?"

Hazel scowled. "He's a real nice guy."

I shook my head. "I'm sure he is." Hadn't Hazel been encouraging me to pursue my heart in a relationship with Ed? Why couldn't I support her as well? Why must I be so quick to criticize? But wait...Hazel, leaving?

I fought the desire to pounce on her with rapid-fire questions. I knew from experience anything that smelled of an interrogation would only backfire. "So, you two have been writing?"

"Yeah, we have. We went out a few times after filming in the summer, you know? I really like him, Pris."

We reached a bench not far from the house and I lowered myself onto it. The cold of the metal went straight through my skirt and stockings to chill my legs.

"So, what's this talk about leaving?"

Hazel lowered herself beside me, shoving her hands in the pockets of her jacket. "I want more than this town has to offer. I want to do more filming. Jimmy says I have what it takes. He wants me to come to New York City so he can introduce me to some people."

"You're not serious."

"Yes, Pris, I am."

"You can't take off to New York with some guy you barely know on a chance for a big break!"

Hazel bit her lip and met my gaze. "I've already made up my mind, but I didn't want to leave without saying goodbye."

My brain stalled. "What—you're leaving...now? You have to finish high school."

"Jimmy says I don't need high school to be an actress."

Something desperate tore at my chest. If I didn't use the right words, the right tone, I may lose my sister. "Hazel, please. Think. This is *not* a good idea. Give it some time. Finish school, at least. You have your entire life to chase your dreams."

"I love him, Pris. I can't wait until summer. I'll die. I have to go."

"What kind of love asks you to leave everything you've ever known, leave your family, and risk your future in a strange city? If this guy loves you, why doesn't he come speak to Daddy?"

"Is that what Ed plans to do?"

I clamped my lips shut.

"Pris, you can't sit there and tell me I'm doing wrong when you're keeping your own secrets. Please, let's cheer each other on. Remember what Miss Thornton said in the movie?"

The movie...oh, *Peyton Place*. "No, I can't remember."

"She said if there's something you want in life to go and get it. Not to wait for anyone to give it to you. Allyson did that. She left. She made it. She found out what she could endure and found her place in life. That's what I want, Pris. And so do you. Let's be happy for one another, okay?"

I dragged in a breath, let it out slow. I had two choices: do as Hazel asked and keep my silence or go against her wishes and tell my parents.

Yet, how would revealing her secret be helpful? Daddy

couldn't keep my sister locked in her room forever. Nor did I want him to.

"I only wish you would think this through more."

"I've thought it through for five months. I'll be gone by Christmas. Jimmy sent me money for a ticket weeks ago."

I slumped on the bench.

"Please, Pris, be happy for me. You won't tell Mum and Daddy, will you?"

I closed my eyes. "No, I won't. You're secret's safe with me. I promise."

Many times over the next sixty years, I'd wonder how things would have been different if I'd never made such a vow.

The naked, frosty branches of the orchards glimmered in the moonlight. I raced past them, the normal fright of the shadows disarmed by the anticipated embrace of the man I loved.

Our tree stood gnarled and tangled, and I could just make out the tall shadow of him as I drew close.

He ran to meet me, catching me in his arms and drawing me in for a kiss. He smelled of wood shavings and Wright's soap, and I burrowed my hands in his warm jacket. His arms came around me, pulling me closer. He picked me up and twirled me around, finally burying his face in my hair.

"I've missed you," Ed whispered.

"Me too."

He found my lips with his own, something urgent and foreign in how he held me tight and wouldn't let go. He drew me in deeper, persistent and hungry. My insides swirled and tingled at this newfound passion.

Finally, I pushed him gently away. "Ed...wow."

He kissed me again. "I'm going to your father tomorrow. I've made up my mind."

The words thrilled and scared me at once. "Not yet—please. Let me have more time to get it in their heads that there's no chance I'll marry Raymond."

He looked down at me, his brow furrowed. "So, they still think you might?"

I hated the betrayal I heard in his tone. I'd been a coward when it came to voicing my desires before my parents. It wouldn't be any easier after Hazel left.

Ed ran his hand over his face and pulled away from me. "I've been conscripted, Pris. I got the letter today."

I blinked, searching out a trace of humor in his tone. "The draft? But we're not at war."

"The draft still exists. I have two years, Pris. I've already thought long and hard, and I'm not going to let it mess up my plans. It'll delay them for sure, but if it's to serve my country, I'm not going to waste time pouting."

I crossed my arms in front of my chest, my legs wobbling. "Two years..."

He placed his hands on either side of my arms. "Am I wrong in thinking what we have can outlast that? Pris, tell me I'm not wrong. I'd marry you tomorrow if you'd have me."

"Oh, Ed, I can't imagine anything better."

"Then why do I hear a 'but' hiding at the end of your sentence?"

"I...my parents. I fear they'll disown me." My bottom lip trembled and I hated myself for not being braver, like Hazel. "If you go off and leave me, what will I do? I'll have no one. I could get a job, but would it be enough to support me? To live on my own until you return?"

Something fell over his features at my words. Sadness? Disappointment? Realization? Who were we fooling that we could make this work?

"Of course, Pris. I understand. I'd never ask you to do that." But his face told otherwise. He turned from me, shoved his hands in his pockets, and looked toward the harbor shimmering beyond the library. "What have we been doing these past couple months, Pris? I—I want to know where we stand, is all."

He was so direct, so sincere—so unlike Mum and Daddy and those in our social circles. So unlike Raymond, always playing games and hiding beneath that smooth façade. I didn't deserve Ed. But oh, how my heart ached for him.

I came up beside him, linked my arm through his. "Ed, I love you. I can't imagine being two years without you—it breaks my heart to think of it."

He swallowed. "Then I'm going to your father. Tomorrow."

"It's no use. He'll never agree. Ed—maybe we should run away. Together."

He lifted a work-roughened thumb to my cheek, and I closed my eyes, leaned into it. "I want to do this right, Pris. Let me at least try."

"He'll tear you down, Ed. I won't be able to bear it."

"If he tears me down, I'll just have to look on our love to build me back up."

## ❧ 4 ❧

*Present*

I blink at the Nativity scene before me, the gesture sending me to the present—to old, weary bones and arthritic fingers. To wrinkled skin and a poor bladder—a posture that makes me cringe.

"Aunt Pris, that's the most romantic thing I've ever heard." At my feet, the lamplight glows off Josie's smooth face. Hard to believe I was that young once. "I can't believe you and Tripp's grandfather...I mean, that's *crazy*."

"Yes, I suppose it was."

"So, what happened? Did he go to your father? And what about my grandmother—Hazel? Did she run off with Jimmy?" Josie shakes her head. "Dad didn't know much about his mother, and nothing about his father..."

Of course he hadn't. I hadn't met my nephew until he was well into adulthood. He'd asked about his mother once, but my silence must have waylaid him from asking again. He'd died too young, my nephew. I should have opened up far sooner.

A knock sounds on my bedroom door. Tripp peers in, holding

a curly-headed baby Amos. It strikes me how the babe resembles his grandfather and namesake. It strikes me then that if Ed and I had gotten together, Tripp would have never been born. Lucky for Josie that the past played out as it had, I suppose.

"Ready to go? We slept a little too long. We'll miss the pageant if we don't hurry."

Josie looks at her phone. "Yikes!" She jumps to her feet and takes my coat from the hanger near the door, helping me into it. "But this does not let you off the hook, Aunt Pris. I need to hear the rest of this story."

"What story?" Tripp lifts Amos up into the air until he gurgles a bubbly laugh. My, that boy is precious.

"The story of Aunt Pris and Grandpop."

Tripp freezes with Amos in his arms midair. "Really? Now that's one I've been trying to get Grandpop to tell for a while now."

"Some memories are best left unearthed."

Josie clicks off the lamp on my nightstand, sending the Nativity into shadow. "And some stories are meant to be told. I think this is one such story."

⚜

I SIT IN THE CENTURIES-OLD PEW OF THE CHURCH, WARM AND content, the scents of pine and perfumes and colognes winding around me. If I close my eyes and concentrate hard enough, I can pretend I am a little girl again, squeezed between Mum and Hazel, Daddy's normally solemn voice belting out *Joy to the World*.

Now, my nephew's wife, Hannah, stands in the back, directing the children to walk up the aisle in their various costumes. When they reach the front, the little ones line up near the altar. I spot Maggie and Josh's two boys in shepherd's costumes, one of their hook's entangling in an angel's red hair.

Once aligned, Hannah signals the music, and they begin to

sing *While Shepherds Watched Their Flocks by Night* in the sweet, disjointed way that only children can manage. Maggie's Davey curls his fingers to imitate a pair of binoculars and looks around the church, acting out the part of watching. I hide my chuckle with a huff and crane my neck, certain it wasn't part of the plan.

In the pew behind us, I catch Ed's gaze. He winks at me, his eyes twinkling beneath those bushy gray brows. I smile and turn forward, my old heart pounding fresh blood through my veins. I chastise myself for such a girlish reaction. No doubt my earlier reminiscences with Josie has caught me unawares. No sense getting caught up in emotions and could-have-beens at eighty-two years old. Life has come and gone. What happened can't be changed, no matter how I wish.

I blink, forcing my attention to the children clamoring back to their parents. The choir stands to sing. Lizzie takes her place at the piano. Amie and Maggie join the other men and women up front. Lizzie's fingers begin to coax the familiar tune of *Silent Night* from the old instrument and the music carries me away to sixty years earlier, to another piano playing *Silent Night,* another set of hands trying to usher calm and silence in a house that is anything but quiet.

## 5

1957

The solemn strains of *Silent Night* floated up to the spot where Hazel and I sat on the top step of the winding staircase of Orchard House. Hazel clutched my hand as I stared out the large window before us, lit with merry candles, betraying the chaos inside the home.

Daddy's raised voice caused Hazel to clench my hand tighter. Below us, in the music room, Mum played *Silent Night* with the fervor of Beethoven. The strains of it competed with Daddy's heated words. They begged for peace on this December night.

*Silent night, holy night*
*All is calm, all is bright*

Mum couldn't stand up to my father in words, but chose to do so in her music. At least, that's what I liked to think. That she was on my side. That she didn't agree with the cruel words coming from Daddy's lips.

"And how does a dirt-sniffing, destitute whippersnapper like you expect to support my daughter?"

"Sir, I have plans to start my own construction business. I've learned a lot the last several years and have a good sum saved already. I'm good at what I do, sir. And I'm proud of it. After I serve my time and my country, I plan to serve this town and their building needs." Ed's voice was strong, sure. I'd never seen anyone so firm beneath Daddy's scrutiny, and I sat in amazement.

Perhaps my father's determination was not the be all and end all of my life. Perhaps I'd been living in a bubble—where his power in our family and in our town made him gigantic in my mind. Here, listening to Ed declare his love for me, I found strength.

This was my life. Why should Daddy dictate every jot and tittle of it?

"Businesses take time to grow. Without the backing of any good breeding, you are destined to fail."

Heat simmered in my chest. Tears started at the corners of my eyes. Beside me, Hazel shook her head and whimpered. I imagined she must have received the foretaste of her own condemnation in Daddy's words.

Below, Mom's playing grew faster, more insistent.

*Shepherds quake at the sight!*

*Glories stream from heaven afar.*

"With all due respect, sir, my parents and their parents before them have nothing to do with how much I love your daughter. Priscilla has my entire heart, and I am ready to do everything in my power to provide for her."

My heart sang at his words and I rose, Ed's surety paving the way for my own confidence. I refused to stand quivering on these steps another moment, pretending I didn't hear what went on below.

"Pris—" Hazel started. I ignored her and launched myself down the stairs before I lost my courage.

*Heavenly hosts sing Al-le-lu-ia!*

*Christ the Savior is born!*

"You're a dreamer, boy. Dreams amount to nothing without

something to back them. And right now, I see nothing. I see a poor laborer lowlife trying to convince himself of fairytales."

*Christ the Savior is born!*

*Christ the Savior is born!*

I entered the parlor, huffing from anticipation. "Daddy."

The piano stopped. Silence encompassed the house. Daddy stood tall before the glimmering Christmas tree adorned in monochromatic, tasteful colors. I almost didn't recognize the slight slump in Ed's posture as he stood near the mantle. I went to him. "Daddy, I love Ed. I want to marry him."

My father lowered his cigarette to a tray on the end table in what appeared slow motion. He extinguished the end of the butt. "Quite simply, Priscilla, your wants are not my ultimate concern. I am your father and I know what's best for you and for this family."

I stood straighter and ordered my voice to keep from trembling. "I'm not marrying Raymond."

Daddy's face reddened, his neck suddenly appearing too tight for his collar. "You will marry Raymond, or I will disown you."

I lifted my chin. I wanted to grasp for Ed but knew Daddy would see it as weakness. "I suppose I'll have to accept that fate then."

A gasp sounded from the music room, but I didn't turn to see Mum.

Daddy drew himself taller. "I'm going to pretend I didn't hear that. Go to your room, Priscilla. And think long and hard about how your dramatics are affecting not only your own future, but the future of this family. You have a responsibility and honor to keep, and you, young man," he said, pointing to Ed, "are getting in her way. If you really care about her the way you say you do, then step aside and let her have a chance at a happy life."

I turned to Ed, trying to speak with my eyes, trying to assure him he was my best chance at happiness. "I'll talk to you soon?"

His gaze lingered on me. Sadness pulled at those gray eyes, the normal storm in them dimming. "Sure, Pris."

I left to go upstairs. Behind me, Daddy spoke more quietly to Ed. But it didn't matter, not anymore. I'd made up my mind.

Once I reached the second-floor landing, Hazel gripped my hand and led me into her room, shutting the door behind her. "That was the most romantic thing in the world! I never guessed Ed Colton had that in him. You either, for that matter."

"I did the right thing, didn't I, Hazel?" I brought my hands to my face, the conversation replaying in my head. "Oh, I can't believe that happened."

"And well it should. How can he expect you to marry that sweaty, pompous banker?"

"But Ed's going away in March. If Daddy disowns me, I'll have nothing."

Hazel put her hand on my arm, her green-eyed gaze sincere. "That's not true. You'll have what matters most. Love."

૭ᏰᏬ

I WAITED UNTIL THE HOUSE LAY QUIET BEFORE SLIPPING OUT MY window. Ice slicked the roof and I slid on my bottom until I could safely shimmy down the drainpipe. I ran from the candle-lit windows into the dark orchards. By the time I reached Ed, his face was an icicle from waiting so long.

"I'm sorry. They stayed up later than usual." I placed my warm hands on the sides of Ed's face, pulled his nose to the warmth of my neck. "Ed, what you said in there—it was the most beautiful, bravest thing I've ever heard. If I didn't love you before, I think I'd have to now. Darling, we will find a way."

He pressed me to him, clung tight and fierce before pulling away. Silence engulfed the orchards and I thought it strange no one was about—not so much as a passing car on the far-off road below us.

"Ed?"

He turned, looked out toward the night harbor. "Your father's right."

I blinked and tried to rearrange his words in my head in a way that made sense. "What? What are you talking about?"

"I have nothing to offer you but dreams. And one can't live on dreams."

I sought out his cold fingers with my own, seeking to breathe life into him, to breathe warmth into the beliefs my father had frozen in the length of a single hour. "One can live on love, Ed. Haven't you said that before?"

"And I believed it. I still do. But love doesn't negate the need for responsibility. And asking you to marry me when I have to go off to training—asking for you to leave your family because I am too selfish to wait to marry you—that is not responsible. That is not love."

"Ed." I reached out to his stubbled cheek. "Ed, look at me."

Those thoughtful, haunting, beautiful eyes turned my way.

"Don't let my father poison your belief. Don't you dare. Don't let him poison our love for one another."

"Pris...he can no more do that than he could keep the stars from lighting the sky. I will never stop loving you. Ever."

My insides wilted with relief. "Then let's be together." I brought his face to mine, sunk deep into him, kissed him as I never kissed him before. I would make him dizzy and crazy with my kiss. I would tease and draw passion from him until he had no choice but to marry me.

I thought my plan would prove successful, for he drank me in, stirring foreign emotions of ecstasy and pleasure to every nerve ending of my body. He pulled me close, and I felt his passion, stirring my own. We could be like this. Forever.

Without warning, he pulled away. "We mustn't."

I reached for him again, unwilling to take his refusal. I'd let him make love to me on the frozen grounds of the naked orchards right here and now. Then he'd have to take me for his wife.

But he set me back again, despite my pathetic clinging. "Priscilla, I will act honorably and do right by you. But your father has a point. What right have I to marry you, and then leave you to fend for yourself?"

I folded my hands in front of my chest, trying to ward off my hurt. "So you will leave me alone to be married off to Raymond?"

He grasped my arms. "No. Never. The thought of you with that man turns my insides. I'd rather die than see you with him."

"Then what, Ed? What would you have us do?"

"Wait for me, Pris. What's two years in the grand scheme of things? When I return, I'll start my business and we will marry. I'll be with you forever, see if I'm not. I'll stand by you every day of my life and protect you always. Take care of you always. Just let me go and do this thing, first. We're not in war. I'll be back and we'll write like crazy. I'll send you money. Stay with your parents. Stay safe and well and—"

"How will I avoid their plans to marry Raymond?"

One corner of his mouth rose up in a smile. "I heard you tonight, Priscilla. You're no shrinking violet. You have gumption, and no one's going to make you marry anyone you don't want to. I believe that with every ounce of my being. So I'm asking you now, Priscilla Martin. Will you marry me when I return?"

I sniffed back a tear. "Yes, you know I will."

"I have no ring, my love, but I saw this in one of the shops downtown and thought of you."

He pulled two figurines out of his pocket and held one out to me. I clasped it, curling my fingers around the hard edges of knobby legs and tried not to laugh. "A sheep?"

"Two sheep. They're from that storefront Nativity. I wanted to buy the entire set for you and for our own household, but I could only afford these. I think it's fitting, though, for sheep are not meant to be alone."

He placed his warm hand over mine. "I will keep one, and you will keep one until they can be together. I'm sorry it's not a beautiful sparkling ring, but it's given with as much heart as the biggest diamond this side of the Atlantic."

"Oh, Ed."

He stroked my cheek with the back of his rough fingers. "We will be together. You believe me, don't you?"

I blinked away my tears and threw myself against his chest. "If only time could fly."

"You will be near my heart no matter how far away, Pris. Remember that."

## 6

*Present*

It is nights like this, with Orchard House alive with the hustle and bustle of family and children and lights and smells and Christmas that I think, perhaps, I'd done well enough.

No, I hadn't married for love. And no, I hadn't had children to fill my days. But in the waning twilight of my time on earth, I find love and laughter filling my childhood home. I'm not sure I could love my own grandchildren any more than I love Hazel's—my great nieces and nephew that fill the Orchard House, now a thriving bed and breakfast thanks to Hannah and her children.

"Do you want a piece of lasagna, Aunt Pris?" Lizzie holds out a plate and I thank her. Her fiancé, Asher, rolls his wheelchair beside me, his own plate of lasagna on his lap.

"Nice to see you, young man," I say.

"Nice to see you, Aunt Pris. Can I call you that, now that Lizzie and I are engaged?"

"I suppose it's only fitting." I remember the doubts I first held over my niece dating a crippled man. I feared such a predicament would hurt her in the end. I hate to admit it, but more than once I see my own father in the way I allow my strong opinions to flow free. In my faults, I try to gain an understanding about my father —try to seek a bond that hadn't existed when he lived. I never quite succeed.

He'd wanted the best for me. However misguided, however wrong—he wanted the best.

Just as I do. Only years of hard life have stripped the meaning of love from my being like a carpenter might strip old paint from a piece of furniture. Along the way, I'd forgotten the most important thing.

"How is that business of yours?" I ask of Asher.

"Doing well. I've been handing a lot off to my team back in Los Angeles, though. Gives me more time for our music."

"And for my niece."

He grins, and I see why Lizzie is attracted to him. Those dimples would knock any girl's socks off.

Out of the corner of my eye, I glimpse Tripp speaking to Ed in the kitchen. He leans closer to his grandson, listening with his right ear, as his left was damaged in a military drill training. He'd written me about it. He'd even been excused from the rest of his service because of it.

Of course by then, it'd been too late.

My chest squeezes and I turn away. Lizzie sits beside Asher and they chat as I chew my lasagna. Strains of *Fall on Your Knees* play in the background, the scent of pine fills the room. I soak it in.

Little Amos crawls into the room, places his hands on my chair. He grins at me and a smile tugs at my lips. I tap his nose. "What are you up to, little man?"

He pulls himself to a stand using the legs of my chair and reaches his arms out to me. My heart lurches and I look behind me, certain he must be directing his attentions to another. But no, there is no one.

I put my plate on the side table, and place my hands beneath his armpits, lifting him onto my lap. "My, you're a heavy boy." I bounce him slightly, awkward, but he giggles, grasping for my necklace—a sapphire pendant.

"You like that, do you? That was your great-grandmother's. She was born the same month as you. Perhaps I will leave this to your mother and you can give it to your wife one day, hmmm?"

"Hazel would have liked that."

I jump at the sound of Ed's voice behind me. Amos wiggles out of my arms and slides back onto the ground, crawling toward Lizzie's outstretched arms. Ed sits in the chair next to mine.

"I forget sometimes that Amos's children are Hazel's grand-children," he says.

I blink, a sigh on my lips. "I don't. But I like to think she wouldn't be against sharing them with me."

His gray eyes twinkle. "I don't think she would have."

We're silent for a moment before I speak. "She's been gone so long. It's nice to know someone else still remembers her."

"She wasn't easily forgettable. Did you ever show your nieces the parts she played in *Peyton Place*?"

"My, no. Although I have a feeling they wouldn't consider it quite as scandalous as I once did." My smile softens. "You know, I think I've taken myself too seriously over the years. Hazel wouldn't approve."

"She loved you, Priscilla."

I sniff. "I've gone down that road as far as I want to go tonight, Ed."

"Ah, but Tripp tells me you and Josie were talking memories before the service. I thought you might be feeling sentimental."

I raise an eyebrow at him. "Me? Sentimental?"

He has tried to bring up our past more than once, but I always cut him off. What use is there in stirring up what can't be changed?

"You have a heart under that puff and fluff, Pris. Don't try to fool me. You're not so very different than the girl I fell in love with all those years ago—"

"Ed, don't talk such nonsense." He is bound to give me a heart attack or a stroke on the spot.

"What nonsense? Why shouldn't we talk about what happened? I still don't know. We are adults, aren't we, Pris? Are you going to make me go to my grave not knowing what happened during those months I was in the army?"

I bite my lip, hard. Maggie's laughter sounds from the other side of the room. Josie and Tripp stand beneath the mistletoe, ready for a kiss. Hannah takes a gift from Bronson's outstretched hands.

"Is now really the time, Ed?"

"If not now, when?"

When, indeed? This night has a way of stirring so many memories. I wonder if God is prodding me back in time for a reason. Is this to be my last Christmas on earth?

My last chance to set things straight?

But going back will only cause pain. I am an old woman now. There are no second chances, no way to do it over. And if I could, would I? Would I have waited for Ed if I'd known what I knew now?

I can't be sure.

## 7

January 25, 1958

D*ear Pris,*
*How are you? I can't believe I'm here, in the Big Apple,
really and truly.*

*Jimmy set me up in a small apartment with a great view. I can look
down and see hundreds of people like ants, coming and going on the streets.
It's the most exciting thing in the world. He says he's working on the
perfect gig for me and has high hopes I'll be starring in my own film by
summer. He said he was talking to Jimmy Stewart the other day and
mentioned me. Jimmy Stewart! Eek!*

*He's saving up to buy me a ring. Kind of like Ed, right? Oh, imagine us
—in a couple years we'll both be married to the men we love, happy as can
be. You and Ed can come visit us in New York. Christmas is the best time
with the tree in Rockefeller Plaza lit up—it's the most glorious sight in the
world. We can show you around—Central Park, St. Patrick's Cathedral—
maybe I'll even have a set to show you by then.*

*I can imagine how hard things must be at home. I wonder if you are
downplaying how mad Daddy and Mum are about my leaving. I've
written them but have not yet received a response.*

*I think about you often and wonder if I've made it horribly hard for you.*

*I say my prayers every night for you, Pris. I think about holding your hand by that big old Nativity set outside our church, and it's the only time I'm homesick. Because more than anything, I miss you.*

*It didn't take much strength to run away, but it takes a lot to stay. I love you, Sis.*

*Hazel*

*February 18, 1958*

*Dear Pris,*

*I told you I'd write as soon as I could, so here I am. Though I don't have much to go on, so far army life isn't bad. I took a train to Boston after going through a barrage of physical and mental tests. Since I'm such a fine specimen of health, I of course, passed with flying colors.*

*A lot of the guys got real drunk on the train. I had a few but wanted to arrive clear-headed and in my right mind. I'm in Fort Dix, New Jersey now, a world away from anywhere I've ever been. I'm processed, immunized, and uniformed. I've been assigned to a basic training company— Company G, 272nd Infantry Regiment, 69th Infantry Division. I won't tell you the nickname some of the guys have given us.*

*I suppose I'm glad to finally be here, because it's one day I'm closer to getting out and getting home to you. Don't get me wrong—I'm going to put one hundred percent into this army bit. I'm betting I'll learn a few things that will help me make something of myself once I get out. I'm bound and determined to prove your father wrong, Pris.*

*I know I'll never deserve you, but I'm going to do everything in my power to try like the dickens.*

*I love you, my darling. With every ounce of my being. Always and forever. Write soon.*

*Yours,*

*Ed*

"Isn't that a wonderful idea, Priscilla?" Mum lifted her glass of champagne to her lips.

I blinked, still trying to comprehend Raymond Hitch's words from where he sat across from me at our dining room table.

Yet, as the seconds ticked by on the grandfather clock in the adjacent sitting room, I began to understand. All too much. "I thought you had a secretary already. Barbara Lind, isn't it?"

Raymond leaned back in his chair. His gaze moved over me, slow and sure. A shiver chased up my spine. He wasn't terrible to look at—most women in town claimed he was a catch. Clean-cut looks, a strong Roman nose, and green eyes that burned with something dangerous. It was the dangerous that repelled me. I simply didn't trust the man.

He cleared his throat. "Barbara is getting on in years."

"She's forty!"

Daddy cleared his throat. "I think Raymond knows what is best for his bank now, Priscilla. He's offering you a job. Isn't that what you've wanted?"

*His* bank. Ha!

I'd applied for a secretarial job at the local insurance agency last month. I wanted to earn some of my own money, save for when Ed came home. I'd filled out the application with stars in my eyes, imagining the look on Ed's face when he came home and realized I'd been working hard for our future, to help him start his business, even.

The stars disappeared too quickly. Daddy had arranged a talk with the owner, convincing him I didn't have the experience needed.

I wondered what made me so terribly qualified for the bank secretarial job if I couldn't handle paperwork at an insurance agency.

I wiped the remnants of dinner from my mouth, the mushrooms and caramelized onions of the Salisbury Steak now souring my stomach. "Would you excuse me, please?" I gave Raymond a polite smile and launched myself toward the door.

Once outside, I breathed in the warm spring air. New life surrounded me—vibrant grass, the flower beds Esther's mom cared for, the white blossoms of the apple orchards climbing the hill—it should stir hope within me.

Instead, I remained detached from the beauty, the turmoil of my thoughts and my life pulling me deeper and deeper into depression.

When I agreed to wait for Ed, I'd simply told my parents that he had been conscripted. I hadn't mentioned our vow to marry. I'd kept the sheep he'd given me tucked beneath my pillow and slept with it every night, holding it close amidst my tears, running my thumb over the small, bumpy ridges of its wool.

I was a coward to downplay my plans, and yet what choice did I have? My only hope was to fend off Raymond until Ed came home. But I wasn't doing that very well.

I ran into the orchards, loneliness gnawing at my spirit. I didn't only miss Ed, I missed Hazel. The few friends I had were marrying one-by-one, leaving me for a world of which I knew nothing. It seemed all the important people in my life left. Might I always be alone? Would this season ever end?

When I returned to the house, the sun dipped toward the horizon. Raymond's flashy Chevy Bel Air still stood in the drive. I ducked into the barn. "Esther? You in here?"

Sometimes my friend would end the night by sweeping the barn. She would sing, her beautiful soprano voice carrying to the rafters.

But tonight, the large building lay empty. The conveyor belts and tubs used to clean the autumn apples stood eerie amidst the falling shadows, but I walked in their wake, unwilling to return to the house.

I ran my hand along the smooth metal of a holding tub,

inhaling the faint scent of apples. Mum didn't do much in the way of cooking and baking, but she did make a beautiful apple pie—something I looked forward to every fall.

Despite how I longed to start my own life away from the firm grip of my parents, I loved this place. The beauty of it, my childhood running around with Hazel and Esther, the ebb and flow of the seasons, and the dependability of the harvest.

"There you are."

I whirled at the sound of Raymond's voice. He stood, illuminated by the large barn door. He moved closer, the features of his face morphing from the shadows.

"I was hoping to see you before I left."

"I—I needed some fresh air. Steak never agrees with me." I gave a nervous laugh.

He smirked. "I'm sure it doesn't."

Oh, if I could do something to wipe that obnoxious little knowing smile off his face, I would.

"Your father is quite pleased about you taking the secretarial job at the bank. I am, too. It's a perfect fit."

What did my father have to gain by a relationship with Raymond and his family? Yes, they had money, but didn't we have enough of our own? What did it matter if money married money, or money married poor when there was plenty to go around, anyway? Our ancestors had made a fortune in the shipbuilding industry. We didn't have to run the orchard—it was more of a charming feature we chose to support for the sake of the town.

"I never agreed to the job."

Raymond cocked his head, stepping closer. Whiskey saturated his breath. He raised a hand to my face and pushed back a curl. "I had hoped...Priscilla, you must know how I feel about you by now. I want to be with you. I want to take care of you. Won't you let me?"

I'd never seen him so sincere, so humble. Perhaps he was shedding his self-assured cockiness to allow me to see the real him.

It didn't change things, but it did cause my guard to fall for a moment. "Raymond, I'm sorry. I simply can't."

He blinked, fast. Surely he wasn't about to cry? "Why not give us a chance, Pris? I've loved you forever." Ever so slowly, he lowered his face. I froze, unable to make myself move fast enough to prevent what he had in mind.

Before I knew it, his lips were on mine, drenching me in saliva and whiskey. I cringed, pulling back, but his arms came around mine, spearing me, dragging me closer.

"Relax, dear. You need to loosen up, is all. I know you'll enjoy it."

His hands clamped against me, pulling me and then pushing me against the rough boards of the barn wall, pinning me between their splintery boards and his solid body. I squirmed, hating my weakness, despising it almost more than I despised what Raymond planned to do.

He covered my mouth with his, his tongue probing, gagging me. He forced my head so hard against the boards I thought it'd split open. I tried to scream, but it didn't reach the air as more than a stifled groan, which seemed to encourage, more than deter the monster of a man.

His hands moved downward, hitching up my dress. His fingers found my skin and grazed unabashedly, moving upward. I couldn't breathe, couldn't scream. Black spots danced before my eyes as I wondered how he thought he could get away with such a thing.

I understood then what Raymond intended. He would steal my innocence, force me to marry him. Would my parents even believe me if I accused him of such abominable behavior?

From behind him, a loud cough echoed into the hollows of the dark barn. Raymond stopped kissing me but kept me pinned with his hands. I dragged in breaths, my world slowly righting itself. Behind Raymond, Esther's form came into focus. Her beautiful brown skin adorned in the blue dress I'd given her as a Christmas gift.

"Everything okay in here, Miss Pris?"

I shook my head, still unable to form words.

Raymond growled. "Girl, you best be leaving this place. Now."

"No, sir. I'm afraid I can't be doing that." My friend's words rang clear and firm. I latched onto them, managing to straighten beneath Raymond's loosened grip.

He turned. "Don't talk back to me, you insolent girl. Unless you want to take her place, turn around right now and pretend you didn't see anything."

I gazed at Esther, begging her to stay.

"No, sir. What you're doing is wrong and I won't pretend I don't see it."

When his hands came off me, I slumped against the wall of the barn. Raymond strode over to Esther and backhanded her across the face. She barely flinched, standing there solid as a rock.

Then he was gone.

I commanded my feet to go to my friend, but instead I crumpled to the ground and she rushed over, throwing her arms around me. "You okay, Pris? You okay? That man's meaner than a wet panther. What's your Daddy thinking, wanting you to get hitched with him?"

I shook my head. "Are you okay? He hit you hard. I'm so sorry, Esther."

"I've been slapped worse than that, Miss Pris. Don't you worry none."

"I don't know what he would have done if you hadn't been here. Thank you, dear Esther. Thank you for not leaving."

"I'm a lot tougher than I look, aren't I?" She smiled at me, her white teeth showing bright in her dark face.

We laughed, but I couldn't hold my smile. "I wish I could be as tough as you," I whispered.

"You're too sweet to be mean. I'm tough because life taught me to be. But it's not always a good way to live. I hope life doesn't

ever teach you to be tough, Miss Pris. It's harder to live like that."
She looked toward Raymond's car, peeling out of the drive. "But I
fear if Mr. Raymond has his way, he'd toughen you up before
long."

## ❧ 8 ☙

I stared first at my mother, then my father, waiting for their expressions of shock.

But they both stared at me, a look of boredom on their faces.

"Did you hear me, Mum? He forced himself on me. If Esther hadn't come, I don't know what he would have done. And then he hit her. What right does he have to strike my friend?"

Mum rolled her eyes. "*Friend*, dear?"

We'd been round these tables before. How could Mum nitpick over who I chose to have as a friend after I'd told them what Raymond had done?

"It's normal for a man to get antsy, Priscilla." My father threw back a glass with shiny liquid in it, remnants of ice chips at the bottom. "You're playing games with him, making him wait so long. How do you expect him to act?"

My mouth dropped open. True, I wasn't privy to the intimate workings between a man and woman, but surely this wasn't the norm? Ed never treated me with anything but gentility. My parents, who shunned movies like *Peyton Place* and hid behind their lace curtains and beautiful Victorian home, were telling me such abominable behavior was normal?

I turned to my mother. "Mum?"

She glanced away, her bouffant hairstyle stiff with abundant hairspray. She'd grown more distant since Hazel left. Slept most of the day. Enjoyed her wine more than normal and hadn't played piano in weeks. My younger sister's absence bothered her, and yet she seemed determined not to admit it. "It's complicated, dear. Why not marry him, already? A man can only wait so long for certain things..."

My stomach swirled, and I backed away from them, certain I'd lose what was left of the Salisbury steak that still occupied my stomach. I turned and walked up the stairs, hearing Father's murmurs.

"She'll see our way of thinking before long, dear. It's only a matter of time."

But I wouldn't. I couldn't.

I threw myself on my bed, digging out the figurine Ed had gifted me, clutching it tight. What I wouldn't give for his arms around me. If I had money for a train ticket to Fort Dix, I would go.

I cried all the harder at the thought of Hazel, miles away. If it weren't for Esther, I wouldn't have a friend in the world. How would I survive another year and a half beneath my parents' roof?

I stroked the hard hoof of the sheep figurine, imagining it alongside Ed's, a Nativity set of our own beneath a humble Christmas tree.

If I accepted Raymond's secretarial job, would that put them off a bit longer? But working with him day-in and day-out—if he acted so abominably on my parent's property, how would he act behind the closed door of his office?

No, I couldn't do it. I wouldn't. But what other options did I have?

I pressed the sheep against my lips, had never felt so lost.

*Sheep are not meant to be alone.*

I remembered Ed's words, remembered the parable I'd heard in church many times of Jesus leaving the ninety-nine to find the one lost sheep.

*God, I'm so alone. Give me wisdom. Show me what to do.*

I continued stroking the sheep, lulling myself into a state of peace, my tears drying on my pillow. I remembered Hazel as a little girl, gazing at the life-sized Nativity scene outside our church on the Village Green. She'd loved it all—the baby, the Virgin Mother, the wise men. But she'd loved the sheep most of all. Particularly the one off to the side, all by itself.

My breath hitched and I sat up in my bed. Hazel. She'd said Jimmy had gotten her an apartment. No doubt it was small, but...

No, the idea was ludicrous. And yet my sister would be happy to have me, wouldn't she? I'd sleep on the floor. It would only be until Ed returned from his duty. I could apply for a secretarial job in the city. I'd save for me and Ed's future in a way I couldn't do in this town.

The idea gained traction in my mind until I pulled a sheet of stationary from my drawer. It could be fun, the two of us having our grand adventure in the Big Apple. I would be hundreds of miles away from Raymond, hundreds of miles away from Mum and Daddy...hundreds of miles away from everything I was beginning to hate.

Perhaps I would do as Hazel wanted to do, as Allyson in her *Peyton Place* had done—see what I was capable of, find my way, and find my place in the world.

❧

I RUSHED TO THE MAILBOX EACH DAY TO AWAIT HAZEL'S letter, and each day I was met with disappointment. My pathetic state served to sink me further, my hopes hanging on my younger sister's ability to help me in my time of need.

Raymond came over for dinner, and I pretended not to be repulsed by him. And although he would steal a quick kiss here and there, he didn't push for more. I prayed Ed would forgive me.

When Mum announced wedding plans for New Year's Eve of that year, I entertained her by not adamantly refusing—which seemed to satisfy both her and my father for the time being. In some way, agreeing to their plans was easier.

Ed's last letter stated he'd been sent to France and there was talk of putting him in charge of troop education. He sounded proud as he told me about the four-hundred men beneath him who would fill jobs involving the handling of the Communications Zone of the Army in Europe.

I was happy for him. Proud of him. One time, I told my parents of all he did. Hoping, praying, they would see something of promise in the news.

They hadn't been impressed.

"Probably lying through his teeth," Daddy said. "And if he isn't, it's not like the army pays anything near what Raymond's worth. Get your head out of the clouds and forget that boy, Priscilla."

At night, I held my sheep close, dreaming of a future with Ed, even as doubts assailed me. What kind of Parisian women did he meet? Surely they were ten times more exotic and beautiful than me. His letters seemed more sporadic, less reliable. And when I sneaked into Daddy's study to look at his globe and saw the immense mass of ocean between me and Ed, I realized the odds stacked against us. With that kind of distance, was it possible for our hearts to still be connected?

*August 3, 1958*
  *My Dearest Pris,*

*I apologize for my silence, dear sister. I don't expect you to forgive it, and yet I pray you will.*

*How lovely it would have been for you come to New York. For us to gallivant around and experience the city together. It seems like a dream.*

*Do you remember when we used to play house beneath the pine trees on the side of the orchard? We'd sweep brown needles up into mounds that denoted walls and fashion out our own homes. We were always neighbors and I'd run over to borrow a cup of sugar—that pail of sand—for my mud cake.*

*I miss those days, Pris. Life was simple. Sure, Mum and Daddy weren't always the parents we wanted them to be, but they loved us in their own way. Tried to do what was best for us.*

*There's something about having a set of walls one feels safe in—whether it be mounds of pine needles or wood and plaster. To be secure and safe are some of the best things in life.*

*Pray for me, Pris. I'm lost. You can't come to New York, you see, because I'm no longer in New York. Jimmy and I drove to L.A. Los Angeles, can you believe it? Hollywood. He told me I'd get my real break there.*

*And he's right. I'm broken. He left me, Pris. I stay with acquaintances here and there. The weather is warm enough I sometimes sleep in the park. I got a job waiting tables and the tips aren't bad. I think about coming home but know I'm not welcome. Many days, I wish I'd never left. Many days, I wish I'd done whatever Mum and Daddy wanted, for surely it's better than living alone and homeless and unsure, day after day.*

*If you write back, send it to this return address. If I'm not here, I will make it a point to check back for my mail in a few weeks.*

*Love you,*

*Hazel*

## ❧ 9 ❧

"I don't know what to do, Esther. Tell me what to do."

Esther tightened her scarf. "You can't marry that horrible being. I've been praying to the Lord for wisdom, but all I know is yoking yourself to Raymond Hitch is likely to be the worst mistake of your life."

I groaned. "I hate being helpless. Sometimes I hate being a woman."

Esther laughed. "Try being a black woman."

I rubbed my head. "I'm so sorry. I don't mean to complain—"

My friend put a hand on my arm. "Friends bear one another's burdens. Let me help bear yours, Pris."

I squeezed her hand. "You are such a comfort to me. Ever since Ed and Hazel left, I've been so alone. I would have gone crazy without your friendship."

"Everything will be okay. I know it. You will find a way to get out of marrying Raymond. Ed will return and you will marry him, and then Mr. Presley will return and marry me."

We giggled over Esther's hopeless crush on the rock star with the gyrating hips who had been drafted around the same time as Ed and had willingly gone to do his duty.

We stepped over leaves the apple orchards had shed last month. Thanksgiving loomed before us. Daddy had invited Raymond and his parents. Mum and Mrs. Hitch planned the wedding while I sat like a delicate China doll, blinking at their plans while slowly dying inside.

I wouldn't marry Raymond, of course. I'd run away on my own first. But I kept putting off such a drastic move, certain some change in fortune would turn the horrible chain of events flat on their face.

"Can I tell you something?"

"Of course."

"I'm beginning to hate myself."

"Pris, you mustn't say such a thing."

"But I do. I don't like the helpless coward I've become. And yet, I don't know what to do about it. Hazel said she wanted to leave—that if there's something you want in life to go and get it. Not to wait for anyone to give it to you. And yet she's alone across the country full of regrets."

I swallowed. "I dream about going to find her with the bit of money Ed sent at the beginning of his deployment. And then I wake, knowing I am foolish. That I wouldn't know where to look after not hearing from her since August."

Esther gazed at me with those wide brown eyes. "If you marry Raymond, you're the one who will be full of regrets."

I saw the truth of her words in those eyes. My future flashed before me, riding on the wings of a loveless marriage. Cold and alone, Raymond flitting from one mistress to another, or drunk in my own bed. Would there be children for us? What would having Raymond as a father mean for them? Was I not responsible for the well-being of my offspring even now?

And what of my real love? What of Ed? He'd vowed his love for me. Why should I doubt him after a couple of slow-moving letters?

"You're right, Esther. I need to stand up to my parents, no matter the consequences."

"It won't be easy. I wish I could help."

"Oh, but you have. You've helped me see what I must do."

Maybe running away as Hazel had done wasn't the answer. Maybe the answer was speaking to my parents.

After dinner that night, I pushed aside my near empty plate of chicken and dumplings and cleared my throat. "I'd like to talk to you both, please."

Mum's gaze fell upon me. Father took his time lighting a cigarette and puffing on it, drawing the smoke into his lungs and letting it out slow. With a lazy finesse only he could accomplish, he raised dark eyes to me.

"I know you both care deeply for my future, but I have to tell you before it's too late. I will not marry Raymond."

Mum rubbed her temples. "Priscilla, you drain me. I thought we'd settled this. The plans are already in motion. It's too late."

Father puffed harder on his cigarette. "Think of your mother, dear. Think of Raymond. You've already promised yourself to him. You can't go back on your word, of course."

He seemed so incredibly sure that I'd *given* my word to Raymond that I paused and racked my brain for such an occasion. But none came. "I haven't."

Father raised his brows. "You can't be serious."

"I have not yet been asked and I have certainly not said yes to a proposal."

The corner of Father's mouth twitched until foreign laughter bubbled up into his throat. He looked at me as his laughter grew. On the other side of the table, Mum caught on, letting out her own slight giggle, almost trying to hide it.

My face reddened, for I had the horrible notion they laughed at me. There is not much worse than being mocked by one's own parents.

I straightened, tried to remember the gumption I knew earlier while talking to Esther. "I don't understand what's so amusing."

"Darling, you are, of course." Father flicked his cigarette against the glass ashtray. Gray ash crumbled to the pristine glass, layering it with soot.

Mum smiled. "To think we're in the midst of planning Camden's wedding of the century and you have it in your head that you haven't yet accepted a proposal. Preposterous! Perhaps you should go lie down, dear. Planning weddings can be stressful."

"I haven't lifted a finger to plan this wedding! I've simply gone along with it, and I'm sorry to say I have."

The smile fell from Father's mouth. "If you'd spoken up sooner—"

"I have told you how I felt countless times!"

"It's too late, Priscilla."

"The engagement has been announced, invitations are in the mail. You're getting cold feet is all, dear. It's to be expected," Mum said.

I clenched my jaw and stood. Yes, I'd been a codfish to go along with things for so long, to expect someone to swoop in and save me. But it was not too late, of that I was certain. "I have not walked down the aisle yet, nor do I plan to. I know it's inconvenient, but it is not too late."

Father's face grew hard. "You will not humiliate us like this, Priscilla. I forbid it."

"I'm sorry," I whispered. "I've made up my mind. I don't love Raymond. I love Ed."

Father guffawed. "That boy is entirely beneath you. If you walk away from Raymond and this marriage, I will disown you as we've done your sister. Don't think I won't."

I swallowed and clutched my used dinner napkin until my knuckles turned white. "While that saddens me, I have vowed to do whatever I must. I refuse to chain myself to a loveless marriage."

Father snuffed out his cigarette in the now dirtied tray. "I'd think long and hard before you make your decision, Priscilla. Once you do, there is no turning back. I mean what I say."

"I have made my decision, Father."

"Then you have until tomorrow morning to leave this house."

"Patrick—" Mum's gaze darted wildly from me to Father. "Let's not be hasty, dear. Give her some time to think on it."

To see Mum's nervousness urged me forward. Surely Father had a heart beneath his hard exterior.

"I don't need more time, Mother. I...will miss you both, no matter how we part."

I turned and sought the stairs as the faint sound of Mum's whimper came from behind. "Patrick, not Priscilla too..."

"Enough, Clara. She has dug her grave, now let her lie in it."

His final words chased me up the stairs. They continued to stalk me and hunt me down as I scrambled for ideas of where I would go, what I would do. It was nearing the end of November —there would be no sleeping on park benches for me.

I swallowed back my emotion, willed myself to be strong. As terrible as the confrontation with my parents had been, I felt empowered, courageous, for the first time in a long while. I had taken hold of my future, however scary.

I searched under my bed for my traveling case we'd used to vacation in Lake George last summer. I wiggled it out and began filling it with essentials—plenty of warm clothes, toiletries, a small pillow, Hazel and Ed's letters. I folded my sheep figurine carefully into a scarf and placed it on top of my belongings before zipping the case.

When it stood by my door, signaling the end of all I'd ever known, I crossed my arms over my chest and rubbed the sudden chill from my arms. I walked to my window where the moon shone over the endless bare orchards. I'd have to say goodbye to Esther before I left in the morning. It struck me as odd that she would live here when I wouldn't.

I pressed my lips together to stifle a sob climbing my throat. I'd start by visiting the church, I supposed. I had but thirty dollars to my name, which Ed had sent. A meager start to our life together, which would not get me far now. Surely, Reverend Daniels would help. My father had spread his influence over much of the town, and while I knew his donations to the church to be generous at times, I didn't think the reverend would deny me help. Would he? Would he not act like Christ and help the lost sheep?

Then again, I was disobeying my parents. Was I breaking one of the ten commandments in not honoring them? I closed my eyes, despair threatening to engulf me. I'd been so certain I was doing the right thing. But now....

When I opened my eyes, I caught a shadow below, scurrying up the drive. Wobbling. A slight figure in a large coat that seemed to hide her frame. She lugged a bag behind her, and I squinted through the glass. It couldn't be...

I whirled, racing down the stairs as the doorbell rang. Voices came. Mum's and...dare I hope?

I rounded the corner to see Mum clinging to a small form. She rocked back and forth. In between her movements, I caught a glimpse of my sister's head.

"Hazel!" I rushed toward them, throwing my arms around both my mother and my sister. The scent of her unwashed body hit my nose and yet I clung tighter. Hazel was home. Surely this answer to prayer was also an answer for our family.

"What is the meaning of this?" Father's harsh voice came from behind.

I pulled Hazel into the house, my own banished status forgotten beneath my sister's joyful homecoming. "It's Hazel, Father. She's come home."

"Isn't it wonderful, Patrick?" Mum's eyes shone as she slipped Hazel's coat from her shoulders.

I recoiled at the sight of the sharp jags of her shoulders and the pallor of her wan skin beneath the ugly yellow of fading bruises. Her hollow gray eyes seemed to look straight through me. Life had been leeched from her. I looked closer, searching for the girl I'd known. My gaze traveled downward and I inhaled a sharp breath at the same moment my mother did.

"Hazel,.." Mum said.

I held my arms out to my sister, wanting only to comfort. "It's okay, dear. You're home now. It's okay."

I pulled her close. My sister didn't speak. Between us lay her bulging belly. Through her thin dress, the babe kicked my own middle. I hugged her tighter as I braced myself for what Father would say. But before he spoke, Hazel fell limp in my arms.

## ❧ 10 ❧

*Present*

It's close to eleven before Maggie and Josh take their leave with the boys. Everyone departs until only Hannah, Josie, Tripp, and I linger by the light of the tree. The Nativity scene is centered beneath it, alongside a small mound of presents for the following morning.

Ed's earlier question dances at the recesses of my mind.

*Are you going to make me go to my grave not knowing what happened those months I was in the army?*

Should I have answered him? There was still so much between us, and my mind seems bent on dwelling on the past tonight.

From her spot on the floor, Josie rubs Amos's back where he lies cuddled on a blanket by the tree. She smiles up at me. "Will you finish your story, Aunt Pris?"

"Oh, girl. It's late."

"Please? I—I can't stop thinking about my grandmother. I—in some ways I see myself in her."

I think of Josie coming home pregnant last spring, broken over her failure and still grieving her father. The family had supported her. If only Hazel's story had turned out more like my niece's.

Tripp stretches his long frame out on the floor, and I see a glimpse of Ed's younger self in the relaxed way he puts his arms behind his head. "Yeah, Aunt Pris. There's nothing that could make this night more perfect than hearing about you and Grandpop."

"Perhaps you should ask him then, young man."

"I have. He said he wishes he knew what happened back then more than anyone. It's a mystery—I didn't realize how much until tonight." Tripp leans back on the area rug, propping an arm beneath his head. Clearly, the boy doesn't plan on going anywhere.

"Okay, what am I missing here?" Hannah inches forward on the couch, clasping her hands over a beautiful maroon dress I've never seen her wear.

"Aunt Pris was telling me about her and Ed Colton. And our grandmother, Hazel," Josie says.

I don't miss the widening of Hannah's gaze, settling on me. "Oh, Pris. I've never heard the whole story. Amos didn't know much about his mother."

"He asked me once, and I put him off. When he didn't press me, I thought we both might be better for it."

Hannah nods. "That sounds about right. I think part of him didn't want to know about his birth mother. Part of him was hurt that—" She stops short, and a stab of regret washes through me.

Truly, why have I agreed to open the doors of the past on this Christmas Eve night?

I sniff, hard. Open my mouth, slow. "He was hurt I didn't take him in."

Hannah comes to my side. "Aunt Pris, I shouldn't have...I mean, he never outright said anything. You know he loved Rita and George. They took him in and loved him like their own. I couldn't imagine more devoted parents."

I bite my lip, think to brush over the comment and the topic of conversation. But tonight seems the night for dealing with history. If I could only make Hannah and Josie understand.

"Do you think I didn't want to take him in?" I hardly recognize my voice, wavering with vulnerability. "Do you think after seeing and holding that little baby boy my heart didn't break to see him handed over?" Foreign tears prick my eyelids. Confound it all. What use are tears all these years later?

Josie wraps my hand in her own. It is soft and warm, full of youth and comfort. I don't pull away.

"I'm so sorry, Aunt Pris."

I swallow. Something about my great niece's words soften me.

I would tell this story, the entirety of it, here and now.

I breathe in the scents of leftover food and pine. The homey scents of Christmas, as familiar to Orchard House as the scent of fresh-baked apple pies.

My bottom lip trembles and words spew from my mouth. "When Hazel came home, I hardly recognized her. She was skin and bones. She looked nothing like the vibrant girl I'd known a year earlier. And her pregnancy was painfully obvious. Father was furious."

## 11

*1958*

M um screamed when Hazel collapsed in my arms. We laid her carefully on the carpet. I slapped her cold cheek gently. "Hazel...Hazel, wake up, dear. You're home now. You're home."

My hands quivered as Mum lifted my sister's head onto her lap.

"She needs a doctor." I looked up for Esther or her mother, for anyone, but only saw Father's tall form standing over us. "Father, ring for the doctor."

His jaw grew firm. "This girl was dead to me when I disowned her last year, and she's dead to me now. Look at her, the little tramp. Went and got herself impregnated by that greaser, no doubt. Who knows how many men she's been with. Who knows what shame her coming back home will bring upon our family."

My chest rose and fell in rapid succession. "Father...you can't mean it. She needs help."

"Patrick, please. We must." Mum bent over Hazel's lifeless body.

I stood. "If you don't call, I will." I started for the telephone, but he blocked my path.

"You were so cocky a short time ago, weren't you, Priscilla? Look what running away can do. Look what damage it causes. You will not call that doctor until I say so."

My ears rang with disbelief. "You're crazy. How could you do this?"

I struggled to get past him, but he clamped his beefy hands around my wrists. I searched his eyes but couldn't find a glimpse of the affection I knew as a girl. What madness possessed him?

"We will take care of your sister after you agree to my terms."

"What?"

"Hazel is no longer my responsibility. But perhaps she can be yours. I will see to it she is taken care of if you agree to marry Raymond."

I released a short breath, disbelieving. "You wouldn't..."

"I would."

"What hold has he over you, Father? How can my marriage to him mean so much you would let your own daughter die?"

"This is for your best interest, and in the best interest of us all. Now, the decision is yours. The power to help your sister is in your hands. What do you say, Priscilla? Will you allow Hazel to perish because of your stubbornness? Or will you capitulate and see reason and sensibility?"

"I hate you," I whispered fiercely.

"In time, you will see I only want what's best."

I wrenched my hands from his grasp. "Fine then. I will marry Raymond. Now move aside."

He did. Trembling, I rang for the doctor, already thinking up ways to get out of my promise.

HAZEL WOKE THE NEXT DAY BUT REMAINED INCOHERENT. DOC Granger said her body was in shock, that she was undernourished and the babe took the dregs of her strength. He wasn't optimistic.

On the second day, my sister smiled at me. I ladled broth into her mouth, hugging her close and kissing her cheek. "Darling, I'm so glad to see you."

"Priscilla." It seemed to take the last of her energy to say my name. I hated how the fading yellow and purple marks along her cheekbones marred her pretty face.

I clasped her hand. "I'm here, dear. You needn't worry about anything. I will take care of you. I promise."

"I'm home." A small smile tilted her mouth. "I didn't think I'd make it. I wasn't sure Daddy would take me back in, especially with..."

I smoothed her hair back from her forehead and shushed her. "You're here now, Hazel. All is well."

"Were they terribly angry? Oh Pris, I tried to write you a million times...I'm so sorry." She began to sob and I feared it would set her spiraling again.

"You stop that nonsense, you hear me? What's done is done."

"I was so stupid. So very stupid. Mum and Daddy will never forgive me. God will never forgive me."

I quieted her with fierce shushing sounds. "Do you remember the story of the sheep that wandered off? The one who left the flock to seek greener pastures? And the shepherd who chased him down because that sheep was precious?"

She laughed, but it lacked humor. "There was no one to come chase me back. No one to take care of me. I thought that's what Jimmy was promising, but I was wrong. So very wrong."

"Whatever you've been through, wherever you're going, God is with you. He brought you back here."

Her bottom lip trembled, and she began to sob again, shaking her head back and forth on the pillow, her dry blond locks lacking their normal luster. "I'm a mess, Pris. Sometimes..." She looked toward the window. "Sometimes I wish God would take me back to him. Take me home. I've been praying that's how the Shepherd will come to me."

A sob climbed my own throat and I lay my head gently against her swollen abdomen. "Hazel, you mustn't say such a thing."

"I'm sorry. I'm sorry to have upset you. Please forget I said anything, okay? I'm grateful to have you, dear sister."

I tried to push her words of despair out of my mind, but they clung to the frayed edges of my thoughts. "Tell me what happened."

She closed her eyes. "I was stupid, that's what happened. You tried to warn me. Jimmy was a scoundrel and I believed his lies. He left me before I found out about the baby. I was going to get rid of it, Pris. But I couldn't. I love the babe already. Is that crazy?"

I blinked back tears at the thought of my sister being desperate enough to give up the life of her child. "You're home now. Everything's going to be okay."

"What am I going to do?" she whispered.

"You must get yourself well first. Your baby needs you strong, so eat up." I lifted more broth to her mouth. She got in half a spoonful before turning her face away.

"Tell me about you. How is Ed?"

"He's in Europe, in charge of troop education."

The smile that touched her lips was genuine. "Of course. And are you planning the big wedding upon his return?"

I set the bowl of broth on her nightstand. "It's early yet. Now get some rest. I'll be back to check on you in a bit."

"Where's Mum? Will she come and visit?"

I bit the inside of my cheek. Mum wanted to visit, but so far, Father had forbidden it. "I will let her know you are awake and asking for her."

"Thank you, Pris." She held out a pale, thin hand to me. "I love you."

"I love you too, Hazel."

I left her bedroom and closed the door softly behind me, leaning against it and closing my eyes, breathing deep and trying to gain a foothold on the entirety of our situation—both Hazel's and mine.

I walked down the stairs. Mum sat at the dining room table, a ledger before her.

"She's asking for you, Mum."

"How is she?"

"Why not go see for yourself?"

Mum straightened and closed her ledger book. "Your Father has forbidden it."

I shook my head. "Is this what you envisioned when you married? Being in chains? Being told you can't see your own daughter?"

I didn't see the slap coming. Hard and fast, squarely across my left cheek, it left a sting radiating across my face. I pressed a hand to the burn.

"Don't you *dare* act like you're better than me. I've done my best and I'm doing my best now. What would you have me do—create discord in my own home as you've attempted to do? I love your father and I will always choose his side. Always. No matter what."

I stared at her, only hearing that she chose Father over her daughters, that she didn't care about us as much as she cared about her fake peace and keeping my father happy.

"We've moved up the date of your wedding."

I turned, slow. "What?"

"With everything happening, we've decided it's best for you to marry quickly. We will hide Hazel here for the time being so her misdeeds do not tarnish your day."

"When?" I whispered, mind scrambling.

"The day after Thanksgiving. Won't that be beautiful? Just in time for the Christmas season celebrations."

I shook my head. "Mum, please. Don't make me do this."

"You chose this, dear. It is for the best."

My knees wobbled. "I don't want this future."

She pulled a cigarette from the pack beside her ledger and lit it, her hand trembling. "Sometimes, Priscilla, the bravest and most honorable thing we can do is put aside our own wants for the sake of another."

I couldn't shake her words from my head. Not as I left the room to return upstairs. Not as I allowed myself to be fitted for my wedding dress the next day. Not as I nodded at flower choices and seating arrangements and appetizers. Not as I prayed with my entire being to hear from Ed, for him to offer me a way out of this mess. Not as I plotted a way for Hazel and I to escape together—somehow, someway, before my wedding.

## 12

Hazel faded in and out of consciousness over the next few days. During one coherent moment, I closed the door of her bedroom and knelt beside her. "Hazel, I want us to run away. Perhaps we can visit the sisters at St. Bernard's, stay with them awhile until you have your baby."

"Away?" Hazel shook her head, started blubbering deliriously. "I never want to leave home again, Priscilla. Please don't make me. Please. Please!"

I ran soothing hands over her head, shushed her quietly. I realized then that I'd never get my sister back—not as she'd been a year ago, feisty and alive, up for anything. What remained was a skeleton of her former self. And the only thing keeping her safe was my upcoming marriage to a man I despised.

As the days to the wedding drew closer, I thought to hire a cab and force Hazel from the house. But before I could summon up enough gumption to do so, her labor pains began.

Esther and her mother attended before Doc Granger came. Hazel's screams punctuated the night air, filling Orchard House, traveling up and down its stairways and halls, where wedding gowns and flowers awaited the next day.

I brought a pan of hot water from the kitchen when I heard the hushed voices of Doc Granger and Father on the stairwell.

"Dispose of the babe, Mike. You understand?"

"Now, Patrick. You know I can't do that."

"Get rid of it. I don't care how. Just make sure it's not seen or known about."

"Father!" The hot pan of water sloshed over on the red carpet.

He regarded me with cool eyes.

I straightened and lifted my chin. "I wish for the babe to be in my possession."

"I'm afraid that's not possible."

"If you wish for this wedding to go through tomorrow without a hitch, it will be."

He relented. "Very well, then. But under no circumstances will you parade this child around. And I'm not sure Raymond will take kindly to it, either."

I was sure he wouldn't. But I'd have to worry about Raymond later.

I realized then that I'd resigned myself to the marriage. If I wanted to save my sister and her baby—if I wanted to keep us together—I had no choice. Perhaps Mum was right, after all. The most honorable thing I could do was put aside my wants for the sake of another.

And while my heart ached for Ed, he fast became a dream to me. Almost a figment of my imagination. Black-and-white where once there had been color. Weeks and weeks without a single letter. No doubt he'd found Europe army life suitable. No doubt he'd forgotten me.

And perhaps it was better that way, after all.

THE CRIES OF HAZEL'S BABY LIT THE AIR AT THE SAME TIME I said my vows to Raymond. As soon as I'd danced with my new husband, I slipped away from the ceremony by wrangling a ride from Roger McClintock. I remembered all those months ago when we'd emerged from the movie theater after watching *Peyton Place*, how I'd found his friendly ways with my sister off-putting. If only she had stayed in Camden. If only Roger was the worst of our problems.

"Would you give me ten minutes, Roger?" I asked as I climbed out of his Hudson Hornet. The crowd at the ceremony would miss me before long, but I needed to make sure Hazel was okay before I returned.

"Yeah, sure, Pris. Whatever you need."

"Thanks." I slipped up the stairs of Orchard House and in through the side door. The house lay eerily quiet, as everyone was at the ceremony except Hazel and Esther. I ran up the stairs in my wedding dress and pushed through Hazel's bedroom door.

The babe lay on her breast, feeding quietly. I wilted in relief.

Esther lifted bloodied hands from beneath my sister and wiped them on a towel. "It's a boy."

"A boy." I grinned and sank into a nearby chair. "How is she? Where's the doctor?"

"As soon as the babe was born he received a call at the Watson's that took him away." Esther swiped her arm against her shining forehead to push aside a stray black lock. "You look beautiful, my friend. I'd hug you, but I'd stain your dress."

I already felt stained, but that was beside the point. I approached my sister. "He's beautiful, Hazel."

She lifted tired eyes to me. "His name is Amos. Amos Arthur Martin."

"It suits him."

Her gaze widened. "Priscilla...you—you're gorgeous. Are you trying on wedding dresses for Ed's return?"

I swallowed. There had been times—times when she was conscious, that I could have told her. But I hadn't. She'd have asked questions, tried to persuade me otherwise. I didn't want the truth to bare its ugly head—the truth that I'd been trying to protect her. I never wanted her to feel guilty about it, not for one minute.

But the deed was now done. I couldn't keep it a secret from her forever. "I've been married today...to Raymond."

"Priscilla...no."

"It's okay, dear. I am trusting we will get on well once we're married." The pitiful words lacked sincerity, and Esther's probing gaze pointed out the dishonesty behind them. I avoided my sister's eyes.

"But Ed...you love him, not Raymond."

"I have not heard from Ed in months."

Hazel's face twisted in sudden pain, and she crumpled over, squelching a scream.

Esther placed a hand on my sister's belly. "Pris, take the babe."

I scooped the child into my arms. "What's wrong with her?"

Esther's face bunched. "She's hemorrhaging. Quick, get my mother and call the doctor back."

The babe began to cry, and with him in my arms, I wrangled with the train of my dress down the stairs. "Beatrice! Beatrice!"

Esther's mother hustled from the kitchen. She dried her hands on a towel. "I left them minutes ago. She was fine."

I pressed the baby into the crook of my arm and shouldered the phone, dialing with my pinky for Doc Granger's office. No answer. Carefully, I lay the babe down on the carpet in the living room and ran outside to Roger.

"Roger, it's my sister. She needs the doctor but there's no answer. He's at the Watsons. Will you find him, or find another doctor as quickly as you can?"

"Wait, Hazel...she's home?"

"Yes. Please Roger, please find help."

"No sweat, Pris. I'll find him quick, I promise."

His car shot down the driveway, and I ran back in the house, only half aware that everyone would be missing me at the reception now, that I had let out the secret that Hazel was home.

The babe released soft gurgles from his spot on the carpet and I scooped him up, noticed for the first time how absolutely sweet he was. I bounced him slightly. "Shh, little one. We're trying to take care of your Mum now. Let's go see how she's doing."

I scurried back up the stairs, saw Beatrice and Esther at Hazel's legs, blood-sopped towels on the floor beside them. The room swayed, and I looked at my sister's face, deathly white, eyes closed.

"Hazel, dear, stay with us," Beatrice said.

"Dear Jesus, save her," Esther prayed.

"What happened? She was talking to us. She's fine…she's fine." I told myself that over and over, tried to convince myself the words were in fact true. I clutched Hazel's babe tight, knelt by her head, stroked her hair. "Hazel, come awake and hold your babe again. Hazel, you must be strong. He needs you. Hazel…" I collapsed into sobs as Beatrice came beside me, probing for a pulse on my sister's wrist.

"Priscilla, I'm so sorry."

I pressed my face into the sheets of the bed, wailing. I gave the babe over and clutched Hazel's limp body to me.

"She was so weak to begin with," Beatrice said, the words no comfort.

I clutched my sister closer, my tears wetting her bedclothes. No. This couldn't be happening. Hazel…surely she'd open her eyes at any minute, make some snapping comment about how boring I was. How I never chose my own life, never chose adventure.

But no. As my arms lay around my sister, her body grew stiff and cold. I knew there would be no more lively green eyes or jokes. No more staring at the Christmas Nativity together. No more sheep.

Sometime in the afternoon, hurried footsteps came from behind, and I recognized Mum's cry. Then she was beside me, sobbing, and I hated her more than ever. She should have been here. She should have supported Hazel, not hidden her in the house and denied her the hospital.

Father and Raymond came later. "The babe must be given away." Father looked as if he'd been crying.

A fierceness began in my chest, stirring up a whirlwind of panic. "I will keep him."

Father laughed nervously. "And what would you tell everyone?" He looked at Raymond. "Surely you don't agree to take this child as your own?"

That's right. I was married. Married to a man I didn't love.

Raymond swayed where he stood. He'd apparently had plenty to drink at the reception. I wondered if he even missed my presence. "Of course not. Be reasonable Priscilla."

I looked to Mum. "Your grandchild, Mum. The only part of Hazel left to us. You would give him away?"

She collapsed into another round of sobs. "What does it matter? What does any of it matter?"

Something within me hardened. I stood, kissed Hazel's chilled forehead. "I will take care of your son, Hazel." I spun and left the room, tearing wilted flowers from my hair, ripping the train from my gown. I sought the back staircase, where I knocked upon the door to the third-floor servant's quarters.

Esther answered, holding out her arms. "How are you, dear?"

"Do you have the babe?"

"Yes, Mother finished feeding him."

I entered their living quarters, cozy and small. Beatrice sat in the rocking chair, little Amos cuddled in her arms. I lowered myself to the rug by the fire, stared into the flames licking a log. "I think I must bring him to the sisters. They will find him a home."

"Oh, Priscilla, I'm so sorry." Esther squeezed my arm.

"Raymond won't take the child. In truth, I don't want Hazel's babe to have any part of this wretched family. He'll have a better start with a loving family, one who wants a child. The sisters will surely know of someone."

Esther brushed tears from her eyes.

Beatrice arranged Amos over her shoulder and patted his back. "You are very brave, dear. The sisters will surely know what to do. Your parents...they will not take him?"

"Father won't. I—I'm ashamed to be a part of them. Ashamed to be their child. And I'm ashamed of myself for playing their horrid games."

"What choice did you have?" Esther wrapped me in a hug, and I sank into those warm brown arms.

"I'm so thankful for you. I have no one, and now I must go off on a honeymoon with a man I despise." I waved off my words. "Forgive me, I don't want to be pitied. I'm sorry."

"You have nothing to be sorry for, dear," Beatrice said. "You know, more than one woman has had the tenacity to change a man. Perhaps you can do that for Raymond. Love is a powerful thing."

I snorted. "Love is not what I hold for Raymond."

"No, not in the sense of fairytales, of course. But he is your husband. Surely, there's something of good in him. If you can find it and unearth it, bring it into the light, water and nurture it, perhaps it will grow."

I inwardly scoffed at her words. I wasn't of the mind that anything good was buried within Raymond.

I stood. "Thank you both. I must take him now."

"Will Raymond drive you?" Esther asked.

"I suppose."

I cradled the child in my arms and carried him to my room so I could change. When I emerged, Raymond waited on the landing.

He swallowed, and I thought he looked unsure of himself. "Priscilla. I know how hard this must be for you."

"I'm not sure you know anything about me." Even as the

words left my mouth, I regretted them. Like it or not, this man was my husband. I wasn't doing either of us any favors by my belligerence.

He stepped forward. "I realize that, and I'd like to change it." He lifted a hand and pushed a strand of hair out of my face. "I'm sorry about Hazel," he whispered.

I nodded, my jaw tight. "Will you drive me to St. Bernard's?"

"Do your parents wish to say goodbye to the child?"

"If they did, they would have been here."

A half-hour later, I handed the babe over, kissing him gently. I didn't give the sister any information, but left only after she assured me she'd find a loving home for the child.

When I ducked back into the passenger's seat of Raymond's car, I blinked away tears and looked out the dark window. He reached a hand out to me and I did not pull away.

That night, he surprised me by not forcing me into the marriage bed. And when I woke in the middle of the night crying, he held me. A week later, he had shown enough surprising care that I thought there might be a future for us. Perhaps Beatrice was right. Perhaps there was a speck of good in Raymond.

If only I could allow my own heart to thaw, perhaps it might do some good.

Ed's letter informing me of his injury and immediate return home came three weeks later, on Christmas Eve.

## ❧ 13 ❧

*Present*

The room is silent when I finish, the grandfather clock bellowing out a single chime to indicate the half hour.

"Aunt Pris, I had no idea." Hannah looks at me, her dainty mouth wide open.

"Of course not, dear. I never told a soul."

"Including me."

I jump at the sound of the deep voice behind me, and turn to see Ed staring at me. How long has he been there?

"I forgot something." He looks at Hannah. "The present you worked on for me."

"Oh, of course, Ed." Hannah stands.

Ed shakes his head, waves her back to her seat. "Not yet, if you don't mind. I think we have some questions for Priscilla."

My face burns beneath his penetrating gaze. "What questions?"

Josie sits on her knees. "You married Raymond to protect my grandmother."

"It didn't do a lot of good, but yes."

"You kept track of Amos, didn't you?" Hannah asks.

I nod. "The sisters kept their promise. Amos went to a family that loved him. After Rita and George died, I reached out to him, revealing that he did indeed have family."

"Did you ever regret giving him over? Did you and Raymond ever know love?" Josie spews out questions as quick as it seems her mind can process them.

I drag in a deep breath, feeling their heavy gazes, conscious of one pair of eyes more than any other. "There were times I wished I'd kept Amos for my own, especially after it became apparent I'd have no children of my own. But most of the time, no. I didn't regret it. Raymond...well, Beatrice was right about him. There was some good in him and at certain times it came out in surprising ways. But I never softened to him. Perhaps that's why he turned to another lady—a lady who would always haunt our marriage. She ruined us. Would have ruined it for Amos had we taken him in."

Josie cocks her head to the side.

"His whiskey bottle, dear. He wouldn't give her up. For that reason, our marriage was a hard one for the near twenty years it lasted."

"Did you ever reconcile with your parents?"

I nod. "We didn't speak for many years, but five years before Father died, I visited. I simply couldn't ignore them any longer. We spoke. It was hard, but old age had softened my father some. When he asked me to forgive him, I told him I did—although forgiving myself has been another matter."

Josie slides closer to me. "Aunt Pris, you did everything you could for my grandmother. If she were here today, she wouldn't want you to cling to guilt. I just know it."

The look in her eyes reminds me of my younger sister, gone for so many years now. For a moment, I sink into the words my niece has just spoken. Allow myself to believe them.

Tripp looks back and forth between me and Ed. "And Grand-pop...you came back and Aunt Pris was married."

Ed clears his throat. "I did, and she sure was. But she didn't tell me what happened. I found out when I came home. My first stop was Orchard House. Esther's the one who told me."

I swallow. "When you came to my house and confronted me, I lied. I'm sorry, Ed. I thought it was the best way not to hurt you."

"You told me you didn't love me anymore."

We stare into each other's eyes and as if from a distance, I see Josie, Tripp, and Hannah leave the room. It grows smaller with only me and Ed illuminated by the light of the Christmas tree, little Amos sleeping soundly beneath it.

"How much did you hear?" I ask.

"All of it, I think. I didn't realize your Father used Hazel to threaten you. Pris, you should have told me. I would have been there for you."

I wave my hand through the air to try and make light of it all. "Oh my, listen to us talking as if it were yesterday. None of it matters now, Ed. We've both lived our lives. You and your beautiful Millie and your child, those grandboys. And me, blessed to have Orchard House after my parents passed on, blessed to have my grandnieces and nephew. I may not have known Amos until he was grown, but he always made sure I was a part of his kids' lives. No matter how crotchety I could be."

"You're wrong about one thing, Pris." Ed's kind gray eyes, hidden beneath bushy brows, probe deep.

"What's that?" I ask, near fearful of his answer.

"We haven't lived our entire lives. Not yet. The good Lord hasn't called us home. He alone keeps the count. We've both been alone for many years. Maybe it's time."

Surely he isn't implying what it seems. "Time for what, pray tell?"

"For us."

I laugh, part nervousness, part foreign excitement. "You've

finally lost your marbles, Ed. I'm eighty-two years old. You're older. I get tired climbing the stairs. I'm not the same person I was all those years ago."

Those soft eyes don't relent. He straightens. "I have something for you. Will you wait for me another few minutes?"

I nod, wondering what in the world he has in mind. On a normal night, I wouldn't wait. It's late and my back aches. Too much excitement aggravates my joints. But then he is gone, leaving me incredibly curious and already wishing for his presence again.

I scoff at myself. I've gotten carried away on sentiment with the memories of this night. I am a fool.

I glance down at baby Amos, the smoothness of a round cheek illuminated by the merry white lights of the tree. From the direction of the living quarters, I hear the others talking. Someone—I think it's Amie—laughs loudly.

When Ed returns, it is with a small square gift wrapped with a beautiful bow. He smells of winter cold and pine. Coat still on, he approaches me and sits at the chair by my side, leaning forward.

"You said you're not the same person I knew all those years ago, but I know who you are, Priscilla Martin. Stubborn, that's what. But I've watched you over the years. From a distance, of course, and then closer after my Millie moved on." He reaches out a warm, wrinkled hand to my own, and I suppress the reaction to pull away. I don't want to pull away.

He tightens his fingers ever so slightly. "You're not only stubborn, you have a heart of gold. I've seen you be good to Esther when she had no one. I've seen you sacrifice over and over again to help my grandson's new family. I've seen you donate anonymously to our building charity, and I've watched you with these kids around. So don't tell me I don't know you, and don't tell me the woman you used to be is no more. I glimpse what I remember of you, and now...knowing what happened back then...it's like time has taken the sting out of what I thought was rejection.

"Listen to me, dear woman. I'm not asking for you to change your way of life for me. I'm not asking you to marry me. I'm asking for us to spend more time together. To not be on guard with each other as we've been in the past. I still love you. The feeling may have changed over the years and circumstances, but my dear, it is still very much there. Please, can we start over?"

I blink away tears. "If you're expecting to make up for what we lost or what we once had, you'll be sorely disappointed."

"I'm not. And you're not going to disappoint me. What do you say, Pris? We could have another fifteen, twenty years on this earth. Why not spend our days doing a little living?"

A slow smile spreads across my face. "When you put it like that, it doesn't sound so frightening."

He stands and bends to plant a tender kiss on my wrinkled forehead. "I thought this might be a fitting gift."

I take the green-and-red wrapped package, slipping the bow off carefully. "What are you up to, Ed Colton?"

He smiles.

I open a white box and dig beneath red tissue paper. I gasp at the sight within. "Ed."

"I thought it was about time it found its partner. It's been more than sixty years, you know."

I pull out a rough-hewn sheep, the figure identical to the one I'd been holding in my room earlier that night. The one Ed had given me as a promise to love me forever.

"I never broke my promise, Pris. Don't get me wrong, I loved Millie with everything I had, but it didn't mean there wasn't a special corner of my heart I always kept for you."

Emotion bubbles up in my throat. "Fool man. You're going to make me cry."

He kneels down beside my chair—not without a bit of effort. "I love you, Priscilla. I thought it's time I told you. Again."

I can no longer keep back the tears. The pain of holding all my ghosts close for so long finally breaks loose. The release of it all is too much of a relief for me to be embarrassed. "Ed, you don't know what you're getting yourself into, but I love you, too." Another sob breaks me, for I never thought I'd say those words to another man again, let alone *this man*. All these years of hardening myself, and here, finally opening my heart up and allowing my own love to pour out. I hadn't realized the depth of such a gift.

I lean over and Ed closes the distance, placing a soft kiss on my lips.

It was different than all those years ago. It wasn't young and full of expectation, it was old and comforting, in some ways the dessert that topped off a long satisfying course.

The grandfather clock strikes midnight.

"Merry Christmas, Priscilla. If God sees fit, we will share more of them with this beautiful family we have."

"Oh, Ed. I do pray so."

The chimes ring out, signaling the birth of Christ, heralding the many wonders it brings. A Savior come for the world. A hope for men. A child who would teach us to love and forgive. A Shepherd to guide His sheep.

"Merry Christmas!" Josie bounds into the room. She looks at me and Ed, her smile bigger than one of Hannah's holiday pies. "You up for some Christmas carols, Aunt Pris?"

A smile twitches at the corners of my mouth. "You know what, young lady? I just might be in the mood for some carols."

The rest of the family pours into the room, most in their pajamas. Lizzie sits at the piano. Josie whispers something in her ear and she begins to play *While Shepherds Watched Their Flocks by Night*.

Josie gives me another one of her broad grins and starts to sing in her completely untalented but joyful way.

*"While shepherds watched their flocks by night*
*All seated on the ground*
*The angel of the Lord came down*
*And glory shone around."*

Perhaps I have made many mistakes in my time. Perhaps I have not done what I should have when it came to Hazel, my lost sheep. And yet now, finally, after all these years, I know a lightness in my spirit born of sharing my burdens with those I love.

My gaze falls to little Amos, still sleeping beneath the tree, reminiscent of the baby in a manger long ago. No one but me knows how much he resembles Hazel, and I picture my sister snuggled safe in God's arms as we sing out the angel's message that there is no reason to fear because a Savior has been born. For the first time, I willingly release Hazel into the care of my loving Father. For the first time in many years, I breathe easy.

Like the Virgin Mary, Hazel had been alone and afraid. And yet, because of my sister's baby, many had been blessed. I look around at the love surrounding me in Orchard House, made possible through Hazel's grandchildren. I see how God has written my story. A second chance with Ed. A legacy that would continue after I draw my final breath.

There is much to celebrate, indeed, and in some ways, I feel it is only just beginning.

Outside, a gentle snow falls upon the dormant orchards. As the grandfather clock ends its twelve chimes and I step into Ed's arms and let him hold me, I see a glimpse of the miracle of Christmas.

And it is more than enough to raise my eyes upward to the everlasting hope that the season foretells.

# NOTE TO READER

Dear Reader,

Can I just tell you how amazing you are?! I'm so grateful for you. Thank you for reading. Thank you for your kind notes and sweet reviews. Thank you for your enthusiasm for whatever comes next from my pen. You all rock!

If you're enjoying the Martin family, I have good news! More books in The Orchard House Bed and Breakfast Series will be coming in 2022! Be sure to sign up for my newsletter at www.heidichiavaroli.com to be the first to know about new books, giveaways, cover reveals, and special deals.

And while I don't have a sneak peek for Book 5 (Bronson's story!) for you yet, I'm including a sample of a dual timeline story dear to my heart, *The Edge of Mercy*, on the following pages. I hope you enjoy.

Wishing you a beautiful and very merry Christmas.

Gratefully,

Heidi

# The Edge of Mercy
## Chapter One

*Swansea, Massachusetts*

I slipped the two rings off my finger to cradle them in my palm. Warm and bright beneath sunlight, no one would guess they taunted echoes of a failed marriage.

I stretched out my left hand and glared at my naked fingers. I couldn't imagine never wearing the rings again, couldn't imagine who I was without Matt to define me.

Sudden anger made me tremble. I'd been faithful. I'd held up my end of the wedding vows. This was not how things were supposed to be. Fumbling with the rings, I gripped them tight with my right hand, prepared to shove them back on my ring finger with force, but they slipped from my quaking fingers.

Time slowed as I watched my wedding rings tumble downward, bouncing a couple times off the side of the large rock I stood upon. I fell to my knees and a pathetic whimper escaped my mouth as I heard the first *clink* against the stone.

My blood ran like ice. I caught a glimpse of platinum, then nothing. I'd have to search on my knees for hours if I expected to find them.

I remembered what Dad taught me to do when I dropped something.

*Don't lunge after it. Stop, think. Let your eyes follow what you've lost. You'll see where it's gone. Then, Sarah, you'll be able to get it back.*

Strange how when I told my parents Matt was leaving me, Dad hadn't encouraged me to stop and think. He'd told me to fight for my husband. He wanted to know if I planned to live on alimony for the rest of my life.

I sighed heavily and stood to take in the scene I'd come for in the first place. The scent of pine and warm earth wafted through the air. Bright sunshine pooled around me, and the massive boulder stood solid beneath my feet. Like an ancient warrior, it offered majestic security, and I gleaned comfort from it. This rock wouldn't betray me. It wouldn't crumble beneath me as my marriage had.

Maybe that's why I came here whenever problems encroached upon my life, pressing in, squeezing tight. Eleven years ago, my neighbor, Barb, introduced me to these hiking paths, and to Abram's Rock. She told me stories of this boulder—legends, really —and though I wrote them off as fictional, I found myself returning here in times of need over the past eleven years, bonding with the sensation that another had indeed suffered in this place too.

Much older now, Barb hadn't been able to make the trip here in years. But that didn't change my attachment to this place.

I looked down to where jagged rocks and hard earth met, swaying before me until I grew dizzy—though likely more from my circumstances than the incredible height of the rock.

I hadn't seen it coming. My husband of seventeen years wanted a separation and I couldn't fathom why.

At least that's what I told myself. Sure, Matt and I had been distant of late, but I chalked it up to busyness—a mere ebb in the many up-and-down waves of any normal marriage.

Yet even Kyle had noticed, commenting just last night on the fact that his father hadn't been home for dinner more than twice in the last month. Not one to bare his feelings, I could tell our sixteen-year-old son was bothered by his absence. I wondered how such a separation would affect him.

As I started down the gentle slope of the opposite side of the boulder, my cell phone vibrated in my pocket. Its upbeat tone rattled the peaceful quiet of the forest.

My heart ricocheted inside my chest at the thought of hearing Matt's voice on the other end of the line. Maybe he'd realized his mistake. Maybe—

I fumbled to see the screen and gulped down the bubble lodged in my throat. My sister, Essie.

"Hey."

"I thought you'd be at the hospital. Where are you?"

I groaned. Calling out of my shift two days in a row wouldn't put me on the director's good list, that was for sure.

I picked my way toward the base of the rock, to where I thought the rings had fallen. "I'm in the woods, trying to find the lost symbols of my marriage."

"I take it you won't be done in another hour or so, then?"

"Ha. Ha." My sarcasm fell flat when I told my sister what I'd done with my wedding rings.

"Your marriage can't be hopeless, Sarah."

I leaned over a hollow area between two rocks. Dead leaves cradled the middle. No rings.

"What's Matt's deal anyway? Did you two talk anymore last night?" Essie's assertive voice knocked against my eardrum.

I knew what she was thinking. Another woman. I'd already entertained the thought. It was one of the many reasons I found myself seeking the solitude of the woods.

"No, and he left before I got up this morning." I'd made sure of it.

"Well, maybe you two can work through this. Lots of couples go through slumps."

Was "taking a break," as Matt put it, a slump? I grabbed hold of a tree branch and pulled myself up the first part of the steep slope, on top of another rock that created a small cave. "Working through a marriage requires two people. Matt doesn't want to work. He wants out."

"Come out with me and the girls tonight. Get your mind off things."

I scrambled for an excuse. "Kyle has a track meet."

"Come after."

"I planned on taking Kyle out. You know, talk things over."

Essie snorted. "The person you need to talk to is Matt."

"I—I'm not ready." This could be worse than a simple "break." There could be another woman. Matt could insist on divorce. My chest began to quake. "I have to go."

"Call if you change your mind."

I hung up the phone, shoved it in the pocket of my jeans, and resumed searching for my wedding rings with newfound exuberance. For what must have been an hour I pushed aside leaves, scraped crevices with my fingernails, stepped back to search for a glint of platinum beneath the sun's rays. Nothing. I sat at the base of the rock and let the tears come.

In the aftermath of my quaking sobs, a numbing quiet overtook my soul.

This place seemed ageless, as though the channels of time sometimes overflowed their banks. It reminded me that many other women had walked these very trails, and I felt certain some of them must have known a pain similar to mine.

&#x6341;&#x2762;&#x6353;

I WASN'T SUPPOSED TO FALL IN LOVE WITH MATTHEW JAMES Rodrigues. Not according to my parents, anyway.

The first time Matt showed up on my doorstep, Dad took one look at his rumpled hair, his Elvis tattoo, and his idling jalopy and told him he could take a long hike off a short pier if he thought he'd get anywhere near his daughter.

Back then, Matt had been nothing more than a teenager with a lawnmower, a shovel, and a good tan. But he had something else —business smarts. He knew how to work people.

He knew how to work me.

He used to visit me at the high school lunch table while all my friends tittered not-so-conspicuously. I still didn't know why he approached me that first time to introduce himself. I wasn't anything to look at. Matt smelled like fresh wood shavings from the vocational shop. His rugged dark looks and persistence caught me off guard.

Before long, I was begging Daddy to change his mind about Matt. He didn't budge.

"Do you think I worked hard all these years to have my oldest daughter marry some trailer trash? And a Catholic at that?"

He said *Catholic* as if the devil himself had spawned the religion. As if half the boys I went to school with weren't Catholic.

"I don't want to marry him, Daddy. I just want to get to know him."

"No. End of conversation." He went away mumbling about how he should have never taken the pastorate position in New England all those years ago.

I snuck off to meet Matt that night. It was the first time I'd disobeyed my parents.

Matt had a Volkswagen with a tape deck. That first night we drove to Newport, listening to Elvis tapes. Matt wasn't like other boys I knew, listening to Pearl Jam or Billy Joel. He liked what he liked, whether it was popular or not.

He liked me.

I'd never known such attention before and I fell. Hard. Every night I snuck out my bedroom window to the end of the long drive where Matt's car waited. We went everywhere the water was, but that summer our favorite place was Newport. We shared our dreams beneath a vast sky. Matt told me about his fatherless childhood, how he avoided his trailer park home—and his mother —whenever he could. He hated being poor and vowed that someday he'd be successful.

My dreams seemed less important beside his. More than anything, I wanted him to succeed. And I wanted to be by his side when he did.

I lost my virginity in a fold of earth alongside the flat rocks of Newport one warm August night. I still remember the crash of the waves, the spray of the surf, Matt's arms around me, his heart beating heavy against mine.

The night I told my parents I was pregnant was the worst night of my seventeen years.

Mom cried. Daddy got so red in the face I thought he'd split open and burst like one of the overripe tomatoes in Mom's garden. He said God would curse me for my sin and if I didn't repent I was on the road to hell. Then he left the house—Mom, in tears, calling out after him.

I felt sure my father went to find Matt and kill him. Instead, he dragged him back to our house, and inside for the first time. I could scarcely look at him from my petrified spot on the bottom of the red-carpet steps.

"You will marry my daughter."

"Yes, sir."

"And you will provide for her if it takes every ounce of your strength. Is that understood?"

I felt Matt's gaze on me and I looked at him, telling him with my eyes I was sorry. I knew he wished it wasn't this way.

"Yes, sir."

And that was as close to a proposal as I'd ever gotten.

Matt quit school to mow lawns and landscape yards full time. Three months later we'd both turned eighteen. I graduated and Matt saved up enough money to rent us a room at the Holiday Inn on the night of our wedding. It was a simple affair, with only my parents and Essie and Lorna, Matt's mother, at the ceremony.

When I lay with him that night, Kyle already grew strong within my womb. I nestled my head in the crook of Matt's shoulder, felt a tear on his cheek.

"Are you sorry you married me, Matthew Rodrigues?" I asked, scared to death of the answer.

He grabbed my wrists and pulled me on top of him. Shook me slightly. "I never want to hear you say that again, you understand me Sarah *Rodrigues?* I love you. I will always love you." He crushed me to his chest. "You saved me, Sarah. You saved me."

I never asked what exactly it was I saved him from. Now I wonder—if I'd saved him so good back then, why was he so eager to get rid of me now?

## Chapter Two

I stared at the pristine quartz countertop of my kitchen. Atop the perfect marbled specks of black and green sat a loaf of bread. I'd taken it from the breadbox without thinking.

I shoved the loaf back into the box with a bit more force than necessary. Matt could make his own stupid lunch. I yanked on the handle of the refrigerator, searching for comfort food.

The front door opened and I straightened so fast I slammed my head on the inside of the fridge. Stifling a yelp, I rubbed the sore spot and closed the refrigerator door too hard.

Kyle walked into the kitchen, dumped his backpack on the floor, then sat at the breakfast bar. "Hey, Mom. You okay?"

Oh, how to answer that question.

I released a frustrated sigh and shook off the hurt. "I'm fine. I thought you had a meet this afternoon. I was going to head out in a few minutes."

"Dad called, said he'd take me. He wants to ask me something."

Ask him? More like tell him his decision to leave his wife and son.

I looked at Kyle, nearly an adult. Lucky for him, he'd inherited both his father's height and looks. More and more lately, I noticed a younger version of Matt in our son. Those brown eyes, so like his father's until . . . until when? Until he'd married me? Until the combination of stress and success had rubbed the shine from them? When had my husband stopped being happy?

I blew a strand of hair from my face. "I guess I'll meet you two there."

Kyle grinned, a shadow of guilt playing on his dark features. "Dad said something about us catching up. Mine is one of the first races, so even though Coach'll kill me, I'm going to skip the rest. Dad has a meeting tonight so it's the only time we can talk."

Behind Kyle, the grandfather clock my great-aunt handed down to us called out the hour with four simple chimes. I loved that clock. Always steady, always consistent, even through the night while we slept and didn't pay it any attention.

"I thought this was a big meet."

Kyle shrugged. "Aren't you the one always telling me family's more important?"

"Okay . . . I'll see you there, then."

"Don't even bother, Mom. D-R has the top sprinter in the state. Enjoy the rest of your day off. I can hang with Dad."

Did he not want me there?

"I don't care if you come in last. I love watching you run."

He shrugged. "Whatever makes you happy."

But I had a terrible sense he really didn't want me to go. Had Matt said something to him? We should all talk together, shouldn't we, as a family?

I brushed off the feeling, tried to convince myself it was only my imagination.

A warm arm came around me and I gave my son a hug, grateful he still let me. When we parted, I tapped him on the top of his chest, and when he looked down I chucked him on the chin. "No worries, kiddo. Go out there and whip those Falcons, okay?"

He gave me a lopsided smile and ran upstairs to change. Ten minutes later he was out the door, his father's shiny Rodrigues Landscaping truck waiting in the drive.

I headed upstairs to the master bathroom, peeled off my clothes, and pulled on some jeans. Who was Matt to dictate me missing my son's race?

I CHECKED MY MAKEUP IN THE REARVIEW MIRROR AND GRABBED my purse from the passenger seat. Just before my fingers pulled the handle of the door, I thought of my husband, certainly in the bleachers, ballcap on, watching our son complete warm-ups.

Something like a soggy tennis ball settled in my stomach. I remembered the last time I'd seen him—night before last. The way he'd stood at the mantel, one hand on it, facing the window. Telling me he needed a break. He didn't want to be with me.

Bitter bile gathered in the back of my throat. I thought of Kyle's not-so-subtle suggestion that I not come to his race, and quite suddenly my hand felt too heavy to pull open the door.

I grabbed my keys back up and started the Mercedes. Half an hour later I walked into Chardonnay's, and glanced around the posh room. A squeal from a corner booth caught my attention. Essie—dark blond hair primped and large silver hoops dangling at her ears—waved from the center of the group of women.

I greeted the ladies and squeezed in next to Jen, Essie's friend from college and now my coworker at the hospital. She gave me a sideways hug, a thousand unspoken words in the action.

My sister always did have a big mouth.

"So she told you guys, huh?" I ordered a chardonnay from the waitress.

Across from me, Mariah reached out a perfectly-manicured hand. "I've been there, honey. I know it hurts like the dickens now, but when he's dishing out those alimony checks, he's the one who's gonna be groaning."

Essie slapped Mariah's arm. "I didn't say they were getting a divorce, stupid."

Mariah stared blankly between Essie and me. "I thought you said—"

"A break. I said he wanted a break."

Mariah raised her eyebrows and grimaced, as if to say, *What's the difference?*

Indeed. Besides a few signatures, what was the difference?

"My friend and her husband split apart for a time and it did wonders for their marriage," Katie said from where she sat on the other side of my sister. "Maybe good will come of this yet, Sarah."

I closed my eyes and shook my head. "Listen, I appreciate you all trying to make me feel better, but I didn't come here for sympathy. I just want to get my mind off things."

They nodded. An awkward silence filled the table as the waitress brought my wine.

"How are the boys?" I asked Jen.

She folded her napkin on her lap. "Let's just say the promise of this night out was the only thing that kept me sane today. Would you believe I left those boys alone for ten minutes outside and next thing I know they're making our shed into their own personal bathroom? Complete with a beach pail urinal." She stuck her tongue out. "I'm lucky I got to it before they decided to do more than pee in it because believe me, that was coming next."

Katie laughed. "At least your kids are old enough to be alone for a few minutes. I got in an argument with my trash man today. He refused to take my trash because it was too heavy. I told him three infants in diapers don't make light trash. He told me I should try cloth diapers."

Mariah wrinkled her nose. "You all are sure making me want to pop out a few. Rick's been hounding me. I can't imagine. I told him no ring, no babies. And truth is, I'm not even sure I want a ring that badly after all I went through with mistake number one."

Essie breathed in deeply, then out. Then again, with dramatic flair. I stifled a laugh. "What's she doing?" I mouthed to Mariah.

"It's some yoga-Buddha technique she's learning."

Essie, with much show, continued her breathing. "T'ai chi. I'm learning a calming technique. When I'm tempted to contribute to the complaints and negative thoughts of those around me, I try to center myself into a state of peace. You guys should try it. It works."

While I embraced—or rather, never contended—my parents' faith, Essie had done all she could to avoid it. Whether through self-help books, t'ai chi classes, a study on transcendentalism, or many hours on a shrink's couch, she tried everything, drinking in each new venture with wholehearted enthusiasm.

"Well I don't know about the rest of you, but I didn't come out tonight to center myself. I came to get a buzz and complain about life." Mariah tipped back her gin and tonic.

Jen flagged down the waitress and ordered nachos for the group. "I'm just happy to go back to work tomorrow and get a break from their shenanigans. We're still short on CNAs though, so chances are I'll be bleaching out bedpans anyway. Beach pails, bedpans . . . I suppose I'm destined to clean urine."

"'The only person you're destined to become is the person you decide to be.' Ralph Waldo Emerson." Essie tossed her honey-colored hair over her shoulder.

"Will someone shut her up?" Mariah rolled her eyes.

Undeterred, my sister put a hand on my arm. "Speaking of making your own destiny . . . maybe now's your chance to do something more than bleaching out bedpans yourself. You've always talked about going back to school, becoming a nurse practitioner. This is an ideal time, sis."

I'd learned long ago not to be offended by Essie's offhand comments. Still, I loved my part-time job as an RN. I didn't even mind cleaning out the occasional bedpan. Besides, now was not the time to find my wings. Now was the time to stay grounded, to fight for my marriage, fight for my family. "I'm still processing the fact that my husband's leaving me. I don't think I'm ready to hurl myself into school just yet."

"Why not? Maybe now's the perfect time. What else are you going to do when you're not at the hospital your twenty hours a week?"

"Remind me why I came tonight?" I said. Yes, I knew I had no life outside of work and my family, but it never mattered to me.

Even now, I didn't need anything else. Didn't want anything else. What I needed was Matt, Kyle, and my part-time job.

Essie crossed her arms and rested them on the table. "Sorry. Didn't mean it like that. It's just . . . you've been living for Matt and Kyle all these years, even for your patients. Maybe it's time you did something for yourself."

Maybe she was right. I thought of the other night, of Matt standing at the mantel of our spacious living room, his hand rubbing the back of his neck, his soft yet piercing words.

*"I need some time, Sarah. Some time away to think. We need a break."*

Suddenly all I'd worked for, all I put my hope in, unraveled before my eyes. Essie was right. What did I have to show for my thirty-five years? An outgoing, handsome son, yes. But what else? A broken marriage? A boxy, three-story colonial? A part-time job I'd originally taken as a step toward my true dream?

I wanted to go back home, climb into bed, pull the covers over my head, and not come out again until God realized I did nothing to deserve this disorderly bump in my otherwise smooth life.

Mariah's face blurred before me. The room swayed. I fumbled for my purse and keys, throwing a twenty-dollar bill on the table. "I need some air."

I stumbled toward the door, my chest tight and my stomach queasy. My life was not supposed to fall apart like this.

I pushed open the heavy black doors. The cool night air washed over me in swift waves. I sat on a bench and breathed deep. In and out. In and out.

"Hey, that's some good t'ai chi."

I looked at Essie, rubbing her sleeveless arms against the chill. She slapped my leg to signal me to move over before she sat. "I'm sorry, Sarah. I didn't mean anything by it. I get it, and you're right —it's too soon to start rearranging your life. You haven't even talked things through with Matt."

I nodded. Ground my teeth.

"Are you mad at me?"

"No. I think I am going to head home, though. I shouldn't be out tonight. I should be home, trying to fix things."

Essie gave me a hug and walked me to my car. I slid into the silver Mercedes Matt bought me on my thirtieth birthday and lowered the window.

"Sometimes things need to break," Essie said. "That way they're stronger when they're put back together."

I forced a smile. "Who's that, Henry David Thoreau?"

"No, that's an Essie Special."

I gave her a wave and pulled onto Route 44.

I didn't want a broken marriage, a broken anything. After I married Matt, I'd worked hard to have my life—our lives—neat and orderly. Essie was wrong. Broken things never became stronger. They weakened, were more susceptible to damage. That's why I kept Grandma Martha's teacup on the top of my hutch where no one could see. If I ever dropped it again, it wouldn't be a single crack.

It'd be an unfixable mess.

# ACKNOWLEDGMENTS

A tremendous thank you to Donna Anuszczyk, Sandra Ardoin, and Melissa Jagears for their amazing writing help and support. I couldn't do this without each of you! A special thanks to Erin Laramore for her sharp eye in proofreading this novel.

Thank you to my husband, Daniel, for continuing to support this writing dream, for listening to me talk out my story and marketing problems, and for being the real-life inspiration behind so many of my story heroes. Thank you to my sons, James and Noah, for continuing to cheer me on. And lastly, to the Author of life. Thank you for allowing me to create in this manner. May any glory go to You.

# ABOUT THE AUTHOR

Heidi Chiavaroli (pronounced shev-uh-roli...sort of like *Chevrolet* and *ravioli* mushed together!) wrote her first story in third grade, titled *I'd Cross the Desert for Milk*. Years later, she revisited writing, using her two small boys' nap times to pursue what she thought at the time was a foolish dream.

Heidi's debut novel, *Freedom's Ring*, was a Carol Award winner and a Christy Award finalist, a *Romantic Times* Top Pick and a *Booklist* Top Ten Romance Debut. Her latest dual timeline novel, *The Orchard House*, is inspired by the lesser-known events in Louisa May Alcott's life and compelled her to create The Orchard House Bed and Breakfast series. Heidi makes her home in Massachusetts with her husband and two sons. Visit her online at heidichiavaroli.com